A DYE HARD
HOLIDAY

AMAZON BESTSELLING AUTHOR
AIMEE NICOLE WALKER

A Dye Hard Holiday
(Curl Up and Dye Mysteries, #5)
Copyright © 2017 Aimee Nicole Walker

aimeenicolewalker@blogspot.com

Cover photograph © Wander Aguiar—www.wanderaguiar.com
Cover art © Jay Aheer of Simply Defined Art—
www.jayscoversbydesign.com
Editing provided by Pam Ebeler of Undivided Editing—
www.undividedediting.com
Proofreading provided by Judy Zweifel of Judy's Proofreading—
www.judysproofreading.com
Interior Design and Formatting provided by Stacey Blake of Champagne Book Design—www.champagnebookdesign.com

DEDICATION

To Racheal Yunk,
You're an amazing woman and I'm so blessed to call you
my friend.

ONE

Gabe

"Whose bright idea was it to buy such a big house?" I grumbled to myself as I hauled four massive suitcases up the grand staircase.

"I believe this house was *your* idea." Josh's accusation followed me up the steps. It didn't take him long to develop the fine-tuned hearing of a parent once we brought the babies home ten months earlier in January.

I would've loved to argue with him, but he was right. I knew

Josh was looking for a bigger space for the two of us to move into so he could expand his salon by converting the personal residence upstairs into a lush—his word, not mine—massage area. I'd fallen in love with our stately home, formerly known as Georgia's mansion, the first time I saw it after rolling into Blissville. Of course, I was living with a different man at the time and never would've guessed that I would live there with Josh and our twins. Life was turning out far better than I could've predicted back then, which meant that I needed to stop grumbling about our parents staying with us, and be grateful our home was big enough for eight people to cohabitate for two months. *Two freaking months!*

That's right. Both sets of grandparents showed up in time for Thanksgiving and planned to stay until we celebrated Dylan and Destiny's first birthday in January. I crazy love both sets of parents, but eight weeks of quieting down our sexy times was just too much. It felt like we just got both kids to sleep through the night and Big Daddy got to come out and play more often with Little Daddy when the Grandparent Express rolled into town the weekend before Thanksgiving. We'd mastered the art of being super quiet during sex with little people in the house, but I was certain our parents would know exactly what we were doing if we snuck off together during the kids' naptime.

"Why'd they have to bring so much stuff? We own a washer and dryer for crying out loud."

"Stop your bitching and I'll blow you." Josh's hushed words startled me because I didn't hear him come up the steps behind me. He was quiet and sneaky like a ninja, but the kind that promised sexual favors instead of killing you. "We're going to have a fucking Norman Rockwell holiday and you're going to behave."

"Or what?" I was picturing him tying me to our bed or cuffing me to a chair in his dance studio to teach me another lesson.

"You'll ruin your mother's first Christmas with her grandchildren." *Damn, my husband plays dirty.*

"Damn you, Josh."

"That's what you said last night when I kept edging you and wouldn't let you come." He sounded pleased with himself, as he damn well should, but I wasn't about to feed into his ego.

"Did you follow me up here to bust my balls?" I asked.

"No, I followed you up here so that I could suck your balls."

I nearly tripped going up the next step, which would've been murder on the instant hard-on he always gave me. "Are you teasing me?"

"Do I ever?"

Josh never teased or offered something he wasn't willing to give. If he said he came up to suck my balls then he did. "But our parents—"

"Are cuddling their infant grandbabies they haven't seen in a few months. Trust me, Captain Comes Hard, they'll forget we exist until their stomachs start to growl at dinnertime."

"Is that why you had that huge lunch ready to go when they arrived?" I asked. Josh's considerate scheming never failed to amaze me. Okay, scheming makes it sound like he is a shady character, which he isn't, but the man always has a good plan in place for every occasion. I benefited from his craftiness more often than not.

"You didn't seem too upset about the open-faced roast beef sandwiches with mashed potatoes and gravy that I served," Josh sassily replied right before he pinched my ass.

"I'm not upset; I'm continually amazed by your brilliance."

I hastily dumped the luggage in our parents' suites then grabbed Josh's hand and tugged him to our room. He was right; our parents wouldn't even notice that we were missing. I closed and locked our bedroom door before I pushed my husband against it and dropped to my knees. Josh wasn't the only one capable of shaking things up a bit. It was my turn to knock him off kilter for once.

I worked the buttons of his fly loose on his skinny jeans, because Josh rarely wore anything as casual as sweatpants, then pressed my nose to the bare flesh I uncovered. Josh's head bumped back against the door and I felt the way his muscles trembled when I kissed a path from his navel to his trimmed pubic hair. I never got tired of the way my husband responded to my touch.

"Gabe," Josh moaned while threading his fingers through my hair. I so badly wanted to pay him back for the sensual torture he bestowed on me the night before, but I was too greedy and had no self-control when it came to wanting him. I knew it would always be that way and that there would never come a day when I didn't need him just as much as the air I breathed.

Regardless of Josh's assurances that our folks wouldn't notice we were missing, I wasn't willing to take the chance. I pulled his jeans down to mid-thigh and went about blowing his mind while I pulled my dick out of my sweats and stroked it at the same pace until we both came. I rested my forehead against his thigh while we caught our breath and our pounding hearts returned to a normal rhythm once again. Josh scraped his fingernails against my scalp and my softening dick twitched like it was ready to fire back to life again.

"Easy, killer," I said to my favorite appendage as I rose to my feet.

Josh smiled wickedly at me, and I was tempted to toss him onto our bed and give him another round, but we heard collective gasps followed by "awwww" coming from downstairs.

"Oh my God! What if the babies took their first steps and we missed it?" Josh asked as he wrestled his jeans up his legs and back on his hips. "You know they've been on the verge lately."

According to our friends, parents, and the baby books we read, most babies didn't start walking until they were a year old. Some babies took longer and a few would walk sooner. Josh and I were convinced our perfect angels fell into the latter category.

Both Dylan and Destiny had started pulling themselves up on the furniture and letting go to balance on their own. Their brazen independence didn't last long before they either fell onto their diapered butts or placed their hands back on the coffee table. We noticed that they had grown more confident and could balance longer over the past few days and were certain that their first steps were right around the corner.

"Fuck!" I jumped to my feet and yanked my sweats back up. Josh stopped me before I could open the door. He was laughing so hard that tears pooled in his hazel eyes. "What?" He silently pointed to the front of my sweats. I looked down and saw that I had splattered cum on the front of them. "Damn it."

"You can use them to clean up the mess you made on the hardwood floors," Josh added, pointing to the pool of cum between my feet.

I stepped out of my sweats and bent over to clean the floor. Josh chose that exact moment to jerk open the door and run downstairs to make sure he got to the babies before me.

I heard him yelling, "Daddy is coming, babies."

"You little…"

I threw the soiled sweats in the hamper and pulled on a clean pair before I ran downstairs to make sure I didn't miss our children's first steps. "Papa is here, angels."

Four sets of grandparents' eyes raked over my body from my flushed cheeks down to my changed pants. The expressions ranged from humor to pride. "I pissed myself," I blurted without thinking. Jesus, my fake excuse was much more embarrassing than the truth. Where the fuck had that even come from?

It was all Josh's fault and that little brat was enjoying my misery. He smirked and pointed to my hair, which I realized was probably standing up all over from his hands messing it up. I felt my face burning with embarrassment as I raised my hands and tried to straighten it the best I could without a mirror and a comb.

"Do you need to borrow one of my Depends?" Bertie asked me after she dried her tears from laughing so hard with the rest of them. "They make them now so that they look like underwear instead of adult diapers. Women's underwear," she modified.

"Thanks, Mom, but I'm sure it was a one-time thing." Bertie loved when I had started calling her Mom, just as my mom loved when Josh started addressing her the same way.

"Better hope not," my father murmured just loud enough for me to hear him. Then in a louder voice he asked, "Why did the two of you sprint down here like we were running off with your kids?"

"We heard the oohs and aahs and figured they took their first steps without us," Josh explained. "Did we miss it?"

"We were just fussing over how cute it is when they say Mamaw and Papaw," Bill said. "They're too young to... Well, look at that!"

We all watched as Destiny took her first tentative step without holding onto something. Her precious face scrunched up in fear as she wobbled a bit then relaxed when she didn't fall. She gave us a big, toothy grin when she took another step and still didn't fall. Dylan, not to be outdone by his younger sister, let go of the coffee table and stepped toward Destiny. He wasn't quite as graceful about it as his twin, so his one step led to two more quick ones as he teetered forward. It looked like he was trying to outrun his fall, which never happened. Luckily for him, his daddy scooped him up before his face hit the floor.

Destiny's eyes widened in alarm as she watched her brother tumble. She looked like she'd had enough adventure for one day and dropped to her butt with a soft plop. Dylan kicked his legs in a fit of anger because his plan had been thwarted. He was such a diva like his daddy!

"Settle down, tiger. You'll nail it tomorrow. I just know you will," Josh softly whispered in our son's ear before he set him on the rug next to his sister.

"Did you teach him how to throw a tantrum like that?" Bertie asked her son before she looked at me. "Keep an eye on those two." She shifted her finger back and forth between Dylan and Josh before she added, "You're looking at the King of Temper Fits right there and you don't need him showing the kids how it works." Bertie went on to tell us some of Josh's finer moments like she was narrating a highlight reel on ESPN's *Sports Center.*

While I never saw my husband throw himself down on the floor and kick his legs, I had been on the receiving end of his sexy, manipulative ways. I loved every single fucking second of it too.

"Yeah, like I'm going to teach my kids to make me miserable," Josh said, rolling his eyes over the ridiculousness.

"No," Bertie countered, "but I can see you telling them to only use their skills on Papa."

I narrowed my eyes because I could see him doing that too. "You better not."

Josh's eyes widened in stunned disbelief. "Why, Gabriel Allen Roman-Wyatt, I would never do something like that."

"You wouldn't, huh?" His Southern belle routine was a big indicator that he was up to no good. He probably already had Temper Fits 101 planned out and ready to teach.

"Okay, not until they're old enough to know to save it for you. I don't want to risk that they throw themselves down in the middle of the store when they're with *me.*" Conniving, but honest.

"You would corrupt your own children to get a dig at me."

"You corrupted my bird!"

"Ha! That foul-mouthed bird taught me a few words I didn't even know," I countered.

"Gabriel, I cannot believe you kiss your babies and our mothers with that lying mouth." Josh's huffy indignation made me laugh hard enough to forget all my embarrassment over our parents knowing what we'd done upstairs.

My mother laughed hard at my husband's antics until tears rolled down her face and she clutched her stomach. "Oh, it hurts."

I could tell Josh was about to open his mouth and say something sassy like, "That's what he said," so I warned him with a dark look that promised some sort of retaliation he didn't want. I wasn't sure what the fuck I would've done if he hadn't listened, because my mind didn't work like his, so I was grateful when he let that opening pass.

We lazed about and took things easy until our friends arrived for our weekly Sunday dinner. It amazed me how much had changed in our lives in a year's time. It seemed like just yesterday that Josh and I were newlyweds awaiting the arrival of our children. Chaz and Kyle had just started to date, Meredith and Harley had just gotten engaged, and Emory and Jon were still pretending that they weren't attracted to each other. Fast forward a year, we were about to celebrate the twins' first birthday, Chaz, Kyle, Mere, and Harley all took the plunge into matrimonial happiness, and Jon and Emory were planning a spring wedding. Adrian and Sally Ann welcomed precious Avery to their family in October and Adrianna was loving her role as a big sister. The Dorchesters were the only ones who hadn't experienced any changes, which they both seemed to appreciate. John had fun harassing the couples with newborns while Deanna threatened to make him sleep on the couch. He must've loved sleeping beside his wife, or his couch was seriously uncomfortable, because he quickly shut his mouth every time she brought it up.

"Do you want me to come over early on Thanksgiving to help with the food prep?" Deanna asked.

"You?" John asked his wife. Okay, maybe he hadn't learned his lesson yet.

"I don't want him to get a papercut when he opens up the boxes of frozen macaroni and cheese," Deanna told her husband. "A true artist like Josh needs his hands to create magic."

I wasn't sure if she meant the food he made from scratch, which was ninety-five percent of his cooking, or his hairstyling skills. In either case, he needed his talented hands to accomplish it. Then there was the sorcery he worked on me, but I doubted the group wanted to hear my take on that.

My cell phone rang just as we sat down to dessert and coffee. I glanced at the caller ID and saw that it was the dispatcher from the police department, which rarely happened after I was promoted to captain. Adrian's phone went off just as I answered the call. "Captain Roman-Wyatt," I said into the phone. I smiled at Josh's little shiver of awareness. He swore up and down I used a deeper tone of voice with my new title.

"Captain, I'm sorry to call you at home on a Sunday night, but there was an incident at Santa's Village," Officer Parks said.

"What?" Adrian and I asked at the same time. I glanced up and my eyes locked with my former partner's. It was obvious that someone, most likely Officer Wen, called to tell Adrian the news.

"The village has been vandalized and there's an effigy of Santa hanging from the flagpole," she replied.

"What?" I repeated. I was cautious about what I said out loud with Adrianna and Dorchester's kids watching me.

"You heard me, sir. It appears that someone is waging a war on Christmas."

"Ho ho hoooooo," Adrian said from across the room.

TWO

Josh

"Ah, someone's excited about Christmas," Al said when he walked into the kitchen the next morning and caught me cooking breakfast to Christmas music. While it was true that I was looking forward to the holiday season more than any in my life, that wasn't the reason I was jamming to "Jingle Bell Rock" while flipping pancakes.

"He's nervous, upset, or trying not to kill one, or all, of us," my mother said to Al before I could respond. "He's been this way his entire life. One year in high school, he was blaring Christmas music in the middle of May because he was anxious about final exams." She got quiet and I felt her eyes on me. "I'm wondering if he's slept yet."

"I slept," I replied with a wry grin. Well, a few hours before my little alarm clocks woke me up because they were hungry. Luckily, I managed well on short sleep.

"Which is it?" Al asked me. "Are you nervous, upset, or trying not to kill us?"

"You've only been here one night, Al. How angry could I be at any of you?" I adored my father in-law, especially when I caught him grabbing Martina's ass that morning. It made my heart happy to know that the Wyatt men remained affectionate and grabby long after the newness faded.

"We don't want to be a burden to you and Gabe," he replied.

I put my spatula down after I turned the banana nut pancakes I had whipped up after I fed and changed Destiny and Dylan. I knew the parental units would be up and at it early, Gabe would have a long day ahead of him, and we could all use a good breakfast to start our day off right.

"You will never be a burden to us, Al. None of you will. We love you and we want you here to share the twins' first Thanksgiving, Christmas, and their birthday. I'm over the moon that you guys got to see their first tiny steps.

"I'm just anxious about the call Gabe took from the police department that had him out late." I had joked about *me* wanting a Norman Rockwell Christmas, but Gabe was the one who wanted the holidays to be perfect. I knew how much he hated working late nights, but I also knew he wouldn't let some asshole ruin the holiday season for our town.

Gabe had tiptoed into our room and headed straight for the shower to either warm up or try to unwind. I climbed out of bed and joined him. He said nothing for several moments, choosing to hold me tight instead of talking. When he finally spoke, it was my favorite four words. "You are my world." I never got sick of hearing it, and I knew that "you" encompassed our children also. Dylan, Destiny, and I were the luckiest people on the planet.

"Good morning," Gabe said as he entered the kitchen. He walked straight to me, wrapped his arms around my waist, and rested his chin on my shoulder. "Mmmm, my favorite pancakes."

"I wanted to do something special for you."

"Any day that has you in it is special, Sunshine." Gabe kissed my cheek and unwrapped himself from my body so he could spend some time with our children before he had to leave.

I heard Dylan squealing excitedly, and I knew what I'd see when I turned my head. Gabe made a big production of stealing a few of his Cheerios each morning, and Dylan would slap his high chair like he was angry, but the giggle that always followed proved how much Dylan loved his morning entertainment. Destiny did her best to bounce her Cheerios off Papa's forehead. She had shockingly good aim and I thought we might be looking at the future softball pitcher for Blissville High.

"I only gave him a few Cheerios to tide him over until his pancakes are done," I warned Gabe. Dylan had a voracious appetite like his papa and got cranky when he was hungry like his daddy.

"What kind of pancakes are the babies getting?" Martina asked me.

"Apple cinnamon," I replied. "I use applesauce as the liquid that binds the dry ingredients together. They love it, and I don't have to worry about them choking on a walnut."

"Daddy makes them healthy, whole wheat pancakes that Papa drowns in real butter and syrup. We make a great team," Gabe said, smiling at me.

"That we do."

After Gabe left for work, I headed out to run my pre-feast er-rands. I felt eyes on me as I made my way through the grocery store adding items in my cart, and I knew damn well it wasn't be-cause they were admiring my outfit, although I did look damn good. They wanted to know what occurred the previous night and were looking for the courage to ask for details. Surely, the husband of a police captain would know the salacious details of whatever happened. They didn't know their captain very well then because I didn't even know where it—whatever *it* was—took place. Hell, I'd probably be the last person to know unless someone else told me. Gabe took his oath seriously and blabbing about an unsolved case was against everything he believed in.

Of course, by the time I left the grocery store, I'd learned enough from everyone else to piece together some of the puzzle.

"Oh my," Mrs. Jamison said, literally clutching her pearls, "it's really tragic about what happened at Santa's Village last night." It figured that the oldest person in the store was the one who finally worked up the courage to pry. My mom always said that you cared less and less about propriety the older you got. I snickered inter-nally because, based on her theory, that meant my mom should be pushing ninety instead of sixty-five.

Santa's Village? That's where Gabe and Adrian were called out to last night? Adrian's response to the call finally made sense then. I thought he was just being sarcastic because the dispatcher inter-rupted our discussion about my annual Ugly Christmas Sweater party.

Mrs. Jamison leaned closer and lowered her voice. "I nearly panicked when Mr. Shoffsky said that Santa was hung from the flagpole." She looked around to see if anyone was eavesdrop-ping because she wanted the exclusive from the captain's man all to herself. "I couldn't imagine who would want to kill old man Adams."

I tried not to laugh when she referred to Mr. Adams as old because she was probably only a year younger than him. I had no doubt that she'd swing her purse and knock me upside my head if I called her old woman Jamison.

"Anyway, I called the Adams's house this morning to offer Eustice my condolences and she informed me that her husband was still alive and kicking. Well, she put the phone down and went and checked to see if he was still breathing. She thought maybe I'd become clairvoyant like that Emerson and had experienced a vision."

"Emory," I corrected.

"Yeah, that's it," she replied then leaned nearer. Any closer and people would think something hanky was going on between us in the frozen food section of the Sac-N-Save. "Even though it turned out to be a life-sized stuffed Santa scarecrow-type thing, if I was your husband, I would keep an eye out on Eustice. She sounded a little bit hopeful when she put me on hold to see if old man Adams was dead."

"I'll be sure to pass that on to Gabe," I told her, trying my best to keep a straight face. "I hate to disappoint you, Mrs. Jamison, but Gabe doesn't share any details about his investigations with me. I didn't even know that someone hung Santa from the flagpole until just now. I don't have any gossip for you." She dropped her pearls long enough to cover her heart like she was shocked that I would suggest such a thing.

"You wound me, Joshua." But not enough to stop her from kissing my cheek. "Don't forget the whipped cream," she suggested after perusing my cart to see what I had picked out.

"Oh, I make homemade cinnamon whipped cream. That frozen stuff isn't good enough for my pumpkin pie."

"Well, aren't you fancy?" she asked with a sly smile.

"I prefer fabulous, but I'll take fancy."

"Go on with you now," she said, shooing me along.

In the dairy aisle, Mrs. Schulman told me that she had seen an older Buick Skylark cruising near Santa's Village a few times but hadn't jotted down the license plate. I couldn't think of anyone who drove the car she described. "Rust spots on the side shaped like the ones you see on dairy cattle."

"I'll be sure to let Gabe know," I said with a smile.

"Oh, I already told that sweet Officer Wen this morning. He wrote it down."

As I was checking out, Mr. Beddinghurst was in front of me and he said that Mr. Adams told him that morning on the phone that he had to close the village early the night before because he wasn't feeling well. Something to do with the sausage and sauerkraut he had for lunch giving him fits. "He took some Pepto-Bismol this morning and is feeling better."

"That's good to hear, Mr. Beddinghurst."

"I heard that several of the shops were vandalized. Is that true? How long do you think the village will be considered a crime scene?" the bagger, Bucky Dillwater, asked me. He sounded a little bit too hopeful, and I knew why. Santa's Village opened in the middle of October and closed on December 23rd. The rest of the year, the high school kids used it as make out spots. I'd done my fair share of using a fake ID to wiggle a lock loose so I could get into one of the closed shops for a little tongue-on-tongue action back in the day. It sounded to me like Bucky, and probably the rest of the kids, were hoping the village stayed closed a little longer.

"Until the captain clears it, Shaggy," I replied soberly. "You, Scooby, Freddy, Velma, and Daphne need to stay away from there because there are serious repercussions if you contaminate a crime scene." I sounded like I knew what the fuck I was talking about, but I got most of my police procedural talk from

The Closer. I just knew that Brenda Leigh would be proud of me.

"Yes, sir." His face turned bright red, and I bet he suddenly wished he was back in English 101 instead of bagging groceries during Thanksgiving break. I let the "sir" shit pass and headed out to my car.

I was down to my final stop and eager to get back home and away from prying eyes and big ears. Luckily, no one at the butcher shop wanted to pump me for information when I picked up my two fresh turkeys and spiral cut ham. I was aware that I was going overboard, but I couldn't stop myself. At least my friends and family would have leftovers to last them a week.

I decided to stop by Books and Brew on my way home to grab a peppermint mocha hot chocolate. One of the owners, Milo, was behind the counter with Emory's cousin, Memphis, who was absent from dinner the previous night. I narrowed my eyes as I neared the order counter. He rarely missed dinner since he moved to town after Emory's brain surgery, so I wondered what had kept him away.

"I'm sorry," he said, blushing profusely. "I was cataloguing my latest haul of comic books for the store and lost track of time."

"I guess it's okay, but don't forget about Thanksgiving. It's on Thursday," I told him.

"This Thursday?" he asked.

My mouth popped open to respond but my thoughts froze. My dinner would be the event of the year and he had lost track of what week it was? I made my turkey gravy from scratch for fuck's sake. *He must really love comics.*

"Just kidding," Memphis said. "I'll be there at two."

"Make that one," I corrected him.

"Got it."

I accepted my coffee and headed over to the bookstore section to see what new releases Maegan had on display. My heart swelled and tears burned the back of my eyes when I saw Chaz's latest book front and center. I had my own personalized copy at home, of course, but I couldn't resist picking it up and holding it in my hands. I turned it over and looked at the photo on the back cover. My beautiful friend had never looked happier than he did in that picture, but I knew it had nothing to do with the photographer, or their photoshopping skills, and everything to do with the wedding band on Chaz's finger.

I returned the book to the shelf and walked over to Maegan's store, Curious Things. She was using her online connections to help me find some special items for the moms in my life for Christmas. I was on the lookout for a rare Janis Joplin vinyl record from 1969 and record player for my mom and vintage Tonala Mexican pottery for Martina. "Any luck, Mae?"

"Not yet, cutie. Don't lose faith; I won't let you down."

"Better not," I said then pointed to her blonde curls she had piled on top of her head in what appeared to be a messy bun, but my trained eye told me she spent at least twenty minutes artfully arranging it to look that way.

"You're not really threatening my hair, are you?" She pointed at the hot chocolate in my hand. "Because two can play that game."

"Touché."

"I'll be in touch as soon as I have something concrete," Maegan assured me.

"So, maybe in time for Christmas next year?"

"Snark ass."

"Oh, I love that one," I told her.

"You're going to love the items I find for your moms too. I promise you that I have a few good leads."

"Too bad you don't have a few good men," I shot back.

"Hell, I'd settle for one," she replied dryly. "I'm not greedy."

"See you next week."

"I feel the sudden need to reschedule my hair appointment,"

Maegan said then nibbled on her lip nervously.

"You know better than that."

"You're right. I'll see you later," she said then winked.

When I returned home, my babies were down for a nap and the grandparents were all gathered on the enclosed porch drinking coffee, talking, and enjoying the gas fireplace.

"You want some help putting groceries away?" my mom asked.

"Nope. Stay here and relax. I'm going to start working on an apple pie to surprise Gabe." I knew apples and pastry wouldn't fix anything, but I was hoping it would cheer him up after what was sure to be a long day.

My mom followed me into the kitchen anyway. "Gabe's going to need it if what I heard is true."

I froze in front of the refrigerator and stared at the picture taken of our family the night Gabe was sworn in as captain. Gabe had Dylan tucked up tight against him in his left arm while pulling Destiny and me to him with his right. He looked so tall and proud in his dress uniform. I loved the smile on his face as I stood on my tiptoes and kissed his cheek. I remember the happy sounds our children made as they clapped their chubby hands. Daddy and Papa.

"What did you hear?" I asked my mom.

"Well, Jane told me that Betty talked to Cynthia, who's married to the coroner who talks in his sleep. Apparently, someone hung a Santa effigy from the flagpole then broke in and vandalized several stores in the village after Mr. Adams closed early due to indigestion from the meatloaf he had at lunch."

"Sausage and sauerkraut," I corrected her.

"Excuse me?" she asked.

"I heard it was sausage and sauerkraut that made him sick. And why the hell was the coroner called out to the scene?"

"The night patrolman freaked out when he responded to the

nine-one-one call. It must've been dark or the effigy was really lifelike. I hope it's not an omen of bad things to come."

"That makes two of us, Mom."

I heard the sounds of my children waking up from their nap through the baby monitor, which pulled me out of my funk and shifted my focus.

THREE

Gabe

"WHAT DO WE KNOW ABOUT THE TIMELINE OF EVENTS LAST night?" I asked Adrian and Wen.

"Well, most of the shops were closed because it was Sunday. Santa's workshop was supposed to stay open until five o'clock, but Mr. Adams got sick after eating his wife's leftovers and went home early," Wen said.

Santa's Village was just a cluster of small buildings at the edge of town that local residents rented each year to sell their merchandise for the holidays. A person could buy anything from candles, quilts, homemade goat milk soaps, to candies and baked goods. The buildings were constructed to look like small houses and were decorated with lights and other holiday ornamentation.

"You sure it wasn't Deanna Dorchester's cooking?" Adrian teased. Poor Deanna couldn't shake her bad reputation, even though we all knew that her cooking was just fine.

"Dude, you need to save your insults for when John is around or else it's not as fun," Wen told him.

"Good point," Adrian replied. "Anyway, so someone strung up Kris Kringle sometime between two and seven when the call came in to nine-one-one."

"Who called it in?" Sometimes perpetrators liked to report their own crimes, especially if their handiwork wasn't discovered right away.

"Mrs. Thompson discovered it after following Mr. Friskies into the village when he pulled the leash out of her hand and took off chasing a stray cat."

"Can I assume that Mr. Friskies is her pet and not a pet name for Mr. Thompson," I inquired.

"Affirmative, Captain," Wen said.

"Of course, she reported a dead body and not a stuffed Santa, so that's why the coroner arrived on the scene before we did," Adrian explained.

"I imagined that it looked pretty lifelike in the dark." I snickered when I thought about Mrs. Adams's phone call that morning. She wanted to know if the effigy was a voodoo doll in her husband's image. She sounded disappointed when I told her it wasn't the case at all. It was a prank, not a death threat or warning to her husband. "Did we find any evidence that connects this incident to the unsolved burglaries and vandalism?" I hated unsolved crimes as much as Josh hated bargain brand fabric softener.

"Nope," Adrian said, sounding just as irritated. "I can't believe there are no security cameras or alarms at Santa's Village, especially after the rash of trouble we had."

"Folks don't like change," I reminded Adrian. "Which means we need to step up our attempts to thwart this asshat before he strikes again."

"You think it's just the beginning, Cap?" Adrian asked.

"Unfortunately, I do. Someone went to an awful lot of trouble for a single incident." I ran my hand absently over my chin while I thought. "This feels like the beginning of something instead of the end."

"Our neighborhood canvas didn't really turn up anything new except there was a Buick in the neighborhood earlier that day that stood out because it had rust spots like a dairy cow. There were also some wild ideas," Wen reported.

"Such as?" I asked.

"The most popular theory is that people are pissed about the village opening before Thanksgiving this year," Wen answered. "It didn't use to open until the Saturday *after* Thanksgiving, but this year the township opened it in the middle of October. That upset quite a few people, Cap."

"You can say that again," came a familiar voice from the doorway. I looked up to see our former captain standing just outside my office. "Knock knock, Captain Roman-Wyatt."

The three of us rose to our feet and greeted Mayor Reardon. "It's good to see you, sir," I told him.

"You too," he replied. "You look good behind the desk. It suits you." I rubbed my hand over the back of my neck unsure how to respond. It felt like my office until he stood in it, then it felt like I was on the wrong side of the desk.

"Captain, we're going to canvas over a few blocks from the village to see if we have better luck," Adrian said. "It's good to see you, Mayor."

"Don't be a stranger," Wen said as they headed for the door.

"It's good seeing you guys also," Reardon told them.

"I have an interview with a potential partner for you, Adrian, in thirty minutes. Do you want to stick around a little while to meet him?"

"Yes, I do."

"Don't you trust your captain?" I joked.

"I just don't want to waste anyone's time. I'll be able to tell in five minutes if he's a good fit for me."

As Adrian's best friend, I wanted him to have a partner he was comfortable with. I wished that could be Wen, but he hadn't taken the appropriate tests to apply for the job. John was a good fit, but the sheriff's department paid better than the BPD. I was tasked with finding a partner from a different police department. Quite honestly, moving to a small town isn't always high on someone's list. In fact, I had only received one applicant once the job was posted.

"Fair enough. I'll introduce you when he arrives." I had a good feeling about the candidate, but I would never force a partner on Adrian that wasn't a good fit.

I turned my attention back to a man I greatly admired once Adrian and Wen left my office. "What can I do for you today, sir?"

"Unfortunately, I'm here on official town business," Reardon said with a crooked smile. "Santa's Village is owned by the township and four of the trustees were in my office first thing this morning asking what you're going to do about the situation."

"You're here to twist the screws?" I questioned. "Surely, you were going to give me past noon to solve this crime."

"I have every faith that you'll catch the Christmas Bandit," Reardon responded with a snicker.

"Christmas Bandit? He has a name already?"

"Yep, which means he'll step up his game to get more attention. He'll get sloppy and you can catch him. You're welcome."

"I hope it's that easy," I replied, but I had my doubts.

"Of course, it's that easy; just ask the trustees."

"I'll be sure to call them if I need additional help from them. Other than this incident, how are things going?" I asked.

Shawn Reardon had never been a talkative man, so I was only expecting a clipped response. Instead, he relaxed into his chair and chatted with me about his new job until O'Malley informed me that Elijah Markham was there for his interview.

Reardon got to his feet. "Well, my work here is done anyway. I'm heading over to the paper for an interview with the editor."

Instead of a formal handshake, Reardon clapped me on the shoulder and invited me to lunch later in the week.

"I don't know," I hemmed. "You can't trust politicians. Next thing I know you'll be asking me to make your tickets disappear when you get pulled over for speeding."

Reardon laughed then said, "Wednesday at noon."

"I'll be there, sir."

It turned out that I had nothing to worry about with Elijah Markham. By the time I followed Reardon out of my office, Elijah had made quick friends with Adrian and Wen. They stood chatting and laughing over a cup of coffee, which allowed me to observe the undercover detective from the Columbus Police Department. He was tall, about my height, with dark hair, a square jaw covered in stubble, and a good-natured grin. He wore dark denim jeans, boots, a pressed, black dress shirt, a gun tucked into a shoulder holster, and his badge hung from a chain around his neck. Quite honestly, the ruggedly handsome man looked like a character you expected to see on a television show.

Elijah Markham straightened his posture when he noticed me approaching. "Captain Roman-Wyatt?" he asked.

"And you must be Detective Markham." We shook hands and I indicated for him to follow me to the office. I glanced over my shoulder and Adrian gave a thumbs-up before he and Wen headed out to extend the neighborhood canvas.

"Adrian seems like a standup guy," Detective Markham said, earning brownie points.

"He's the best," I replied. "Tell me a little bit about yourself and why you think Blissville would be a good fit for you."

"Well, I did eight years in the military right after high school—most of it spent in combat—then pursued a degree in criminal justice before I applied for the police academy. I was promoted through the ranks in Columbus at a fairly quick pace and jumped on my first opportunity to make detective. I probably should've thought it over a little longer because undercover vice was never my dream job and it seems the only way out is for me to transfer." I had seen that with my own eyes and knew he spoke the truth.

"Tell me something about you that I won't find in here." I rapped my knuckles against the file that contained his employment history sitting on my desk. I saw his aptitude tests, his psychological exams, reports that extolled his accuracy with a firearm, and several commendations from when he was a patrol officer that told me he'd pull his weapon as a last resort. He was the kind of guy I wanted on my team.

"I had a four eighty-five batting average the last year I played on the police department softball team."

"How long ago was that?"

"Two years, sir. I just couldn't work it into my schedule when I was working undercover in a motorcycle gang," Detective Markham said.

I'd known many undercover cops who took the wrong paths in life for a multitude of reasons. Most of them were placed in unfathomable conditions and often had to make some dicey decisions. Doing the right thing could get you killed. To some, staying alive meant crossing a line and justifying their actions without regard for those they hurt. I only wanted individuals with the highest integrity on my police force. I looked him square in the eyes and asked, "When you look at yourself in the mirror each night, what do you see?"

"A man who is proud of his service—both to his country and to the citizens I have sworn to protect. I see a man who knows the right decision is often the hardest, and I'm not afraid to make it. I'm a man who goes to sleep with a clear conscience, sir."

"I think you'd make a great fit here, Detective Markham. Are you sure moving to Blissville is what you want?"

"I discarded the posting more than a dozen times, but I kept coming back to it. It just feels right to me."

"I'm glad you feel that way because I think you'd make a fine addition to our team. I'd like to offer you the position."

"Thank you, sir. I'm grateful for the opportunity, but I need to be upfront and tell you that I won't be able to start until I can wrap up my current undercover case. I'd love to tell you that it will only be a few weeks, but…"

"I understand, Detective Markham. I have no desire to undermine your case or put another officer in harm's way by pulling you off a case too soon. I know how deep in cover you have to go sometimes. The position is yours."

"I'm honored." He reached across my desk and shook my hand.

"Welcome to Blissville, Detective Markham."

Warmth, laughter, and the delicious aroma of baked apple pie greeted me when I stepped inside our home. An easy smile spread across my face because I loved my life. No matter how tough my work day was, I got to come home to my beautiful family. My smile turned into delighted laughter when Destiny and Dylan squealed happily when I walked into the family room. I squatted down, opened my arms, and held my breath when they both toddled toward me a few steps before falling down on their butts. Dylan started to cry, and I'm pretty sure Destiny rolled her eyes at his theatrics.

I scooped them both up and cradled them against my chest. "Did you miss Papa?"

"Paaaapa!" they both chanted.

"I missed you too." I kissed them each on top of their heads then accepted Josh's welcome home kiss. "So, what did you guys do today?"

"The town folk tried to pump me for information about the crime committed at Santa's Village," Josh informed me.

"What did you tell them?"

"I told them I needed more time to work the scoop out of you."

I laughed then asked, "Is that why you baked a pie?"

"No, I figured you could use comfort food after a long day," Josh responded then stood on his tiptoes and leaned closer so that his lips touched my ear. "I'll bring out the heavy guns later to get the information out of you."

"Cuffs? Rope? Your favorite burgundy silk tie?"

"I was thinking more like a scalp massage, perv."

I followed him into the kitchen, admiring his round ass every step of the way. I had big plans for him after the babies and grandparents went to sleep for the night. Until then, I kept my mind out of the gutter and listened as he talked about his day while I fed the twins. Of course, I got held up on the part where he talked about it being a make out spot for teens during off season.

"Which you don't know from personal experience though, right?" I asked.

"Ummm."

"Sunshine?"

He turned around slowly, his fingers coated in egg and flour from battering the country fried steaks. "Baby, you knew I wasn't a virgin when we met."

"How often?"

"Really, Gabe?" He rolled his eyes and turned back to his task. "I was like every horny misfit who wanted to find affection and acceptance any way he could. It was just sex and I usually felt pretty shitty afterward." Josh paused for a second then added, "I can't regret it though, because it sure makes me appreciate what I have with you."

"Who were they?" Yeah, two years later, and I was still dragging my knuckles. "Never mind; I don't want to know."

"I wasn't going to tell you anyway." Josh laughed then changed the subject. "Tell me about the parts of your day that you can share."

"You won't believe it," I said, using a familiar phrase.

"Try me."

"I hired a new partner for Adrian," I announced.

"How did that feel?"

"What do you mean?"

"Are you worried that he's going to replace you in Adrian's life?" Josh asked.

"I hadn't even thought about it." *Until now.* I had expected things to get a little awkward when I was promoted as Adrian's supervisor, even though it was his idea, but it never happened. Things had been blissfully slow in Blissville and not a lot of investigating was required until someone decided to hang Santa from a flagpole. The burglary and vandalism cases from the previous year had gone cold. Was this the same person starting back up again, or was this a new threat to our community?

The grandmas snatched my children away from me before I could take them upstairs for their nightly bath. Josh chuckled at my scowl and pointed toward the newspaper folded neatly on the table. "Why don't you make the most of it and read the paper since you didn't get the chance to this morning."

"Where's my glass of sherry, pipe, and slippers?" I asked.

"The fifties are calling and they want their Neanderthal back," Josh replied sassily.

"You love it when I go caveman on you."

"Yes, in bed. You just keep it up and see where it gets you."

"Oh, are you threatening to withhold sex again? I wonder if you can make it past ten minutes this time." I scanned the front page and didn't see anything too interesting. I opened to the second page and all my good humor vanished when I saw a smug, smiling face of a man I wanted to punch. "Did you know about this?"

"Can you be more specific, dear?"

"Did you know your *ex-lover* is the newest resident at Blissville Family Medicine?"

"Uh, I might've seen something about it on their Facebook page last week."

"Last week?" I asked hotly. "When were you going to tell me?"

Josh snorted and said, "I was hoping for never." My husband washed and dried his hands before he turned to look at me. "He won't last long around here, babe. He's a big city boy not suited for a small town. He'll get bored and move on to someplace else. I didn't see the need to upset you."

"Of all the places he could've gone, he chose your hometown?"

Josh shrugged. "It doesn't really matter though, does it? He's not you." Josh returned back to his beloved stove and lowered the battered meat into the hot oil. To him, the conversation was over, but my mind was still rolling the new information as I processed it from every angle.

"When is Dylan and Destiny's next checkup?" I asked.

"January," Josh answered. "Trust me, Trent will be long gone by then."

I wanted to believe Josh, but I was a big city guy who loved the change of pace in a small town. Plus, I found the love of my life in this tiny town. Doctor Douche would just need to cast his eyes in another direction because Josh Roman-Wyatt was off the market.

FOUR

Josh

I HAD LEARNED THE FIRST YEAR OF BUSINESS THAT IT MADE NO sense to keep the salon doors open the week of Thanksgiving. Very few people were thinking about their hair on the Tuesday or Wednesday before turkey day, and they were all shopping on the Friday and Saturday after. It became known as Josh's mini vacation and my favorite time of the year.

The grandmas went out to do some shopping with an ornery gleam in their eyes that made me nervous, while my dad took Al to the VFW to introduce him to some of his old poker buddies. Gabe had a crime to solve so that left me blissfully alone with my babies and pets. Before Gabe and the babies, I'd enjoy a leisurely pumpkin spice latte and pumpkin nut muffin at The Brew on Tuesdays before the holiday to enjoy the calm before the storm. Fast forward a freakishly short period of time and my life was completely different. I still sipped a pumpkin spice latte and ate a pumpkin nut muffin, but they were brought to my house by my best friends and consumed fast before the twins could find too much mischief.

Mere squatted down and held her arms open wide. "Come show Auntie Mere how fast you're growing up." Dylan and Destiny squealed in delight at the sight of our visitors and were too excited to get many steps in before gravity won the battle. Mere scooped them up and held them tight against her chest and kissed their round, rosy cheeks clean off.

"Leave some cheeks for me to kiss," Chaz playfully whined.

"I have a cheek you can kiss," Mere retorted, but she passed Destiny and Dylan to Chaz.

My Mere always wore a smile on her face. In fact, it was impossible to know if she was upset about something until she chose the time to reveal it to you. The smile she wore that morning was just as brilliant, but there was a slyness to it that told me Meredith Richmond-Sutherland had a secret. I narrowed my eyes as I studied her. She declined caffeine and was sipping ginger ale instead. I suspected I knew exactly what her secret was too. The old Josh would've blurted out his suspicions right away, but the new Josh was mature and knew it was better not to ruin Meredith's big moment.

"Have you guys heard any gossip around town about the Christmas Bandit?" I asked my friends, referring to the headline I saw in the paper that morning.

"Ho ho ho!" Savage screeched. I suspected he was insulting us rather than imitating Santa, but I chose not to call him on it. He was making an effort to clean up his act.

"Gobble gobble gobble," Sassy replied. They sounded like an old married couple. Savage would say something and Sassy would either join in or contradict him depending on her mood.

Chaz snorted. "Plenty of gossip, but none of it sounds practical."

"Which is your favorite theory, Chaz?" Mere asked him.

"That someone vandalized Santa's Village because it opened before Thanksgiving this year."

"Things are getting out of control. I saw Halloween candy on shelves at the end of July!" I told them.

"Leave it to you guys to be practical in your theories. I'm going with the alien theory," Mere said with a smirk. She loved her sci-fi movies and television shows, so her choice wasn't a surprise.

"Gabe discovered last night that Trenton is doing a rotation at our pediatrician's office," I told my friends.

"How'd that go over?" Chaz asked.

"I'm thinking about as well as a lead balloon," Mere added.

"Pretty much," I conceded. "He wasn't happy that I didn't tell him and was suspicious why I chose to keep that tidbit to myself." I smiled at the memory of the way he imprinted upon me that I belonged to him and no one else. I tugged on the sleeves at my wrist to make sure the slight marks his handcuffs left behind remained hidden. Gabe was horrified that he'd gotten carried away, but not me. I caught myself running my fingers over the abraded skin and thinking back to the way Gabe captured my ecstatic cries in his mouth so that I didn't wake our parents.

"Let me guess," Chaz said, "he wants you to find a new pediatrician."

I nodded my head. "He did say something about that, but I assured him that Trent would get tired of small-town life soon enough and be on his way. I made a bet with Gabe that he'd move on before the babies' next checkup appointment in January."

Chaz and Mere looked at one another, sharing a grimace.

"What?" I asked

"I hope you didn't make a big wager because I'm pretty sure I saw Kyle's real estate agent showing Trent a house in our neighborhood," Mere said. "He looks to me like he's digging in, not bugging out."

"Fuck," I said under my breath so that my children didn't hear me.

"What will you lose if he stays?" Chaz asked.

"My sanity."

"You bet your sanity that Trent would move on?" Chaz shook his head in disbelief. "I know you got more creative than that. Naughty sexual favors?"

"Oh, stop! He'd lose that bet on purpose," Mere told Chaz.

"Okay, technically it wasn't a bet. It was more like a cocky statement that I know Gabe won't let me back down from."

After my friends left, I sprawled on the rug and let my babies crawl all over me while they giggled. Buddy joined me and lay patiently while the twins cuddled up next to him where they eventually fell asleep on his chest. They looked so peaceful that I didn't want to disturb them, but I knew Buddy couldn't be comfortable, so I risked ruining naptime by moving them to their beds.

When we first brought Dylan and Destiny home, they got fussy when we put them in separate cribs. They were used to sharing a tight space and both appeared to feel lost without their sibling near. They quieted and became peaceful the second we put them in the same crib, and we decided that they'd let us know when they wanted their own individual space. Ten months later, Destiny still reached for her big brother as she drifted to sleep beside him. It was quiet moments like those, little snapshots in time, that were so beautiful that my chest hurt from the tight hold my angels had on my heart. I wished that I could slow down time because they were growing up so damn fast. Before I knew it, they'd be starting preschool. That was more than I could handle, so I went back downstairs and grabbed a sketch pad and began planning my surprise for Gabe.

"Wait until you see what we bought," my mom said when they returned a few hours later. She and Martina proudly held up their shopping bags and my suspicions from earlier returned. "Josh, knock that off," she said after I groaned. "Ugly Christmas sweaters? Pilgrim costumes? What have you done, Mother?"

"Don't be silly," she said, waving her free hand at me before she reached inside the bag and pulled out a pair of red and black flannel pajama pants and a red Henley style pajama top with a snowman embroidered on it. "Matching pajamas for Christmas Eve for the entire family. We'll have our pictures taken by the big fireplace in the formal living room."

"A new family tradition," Martina added, grinning broadly. I could see where Gabe got his love for the holidays. "I'm worried that Gabriel is going to hate this, so I'm counting on your help, Josh."

I was pretty certain that Gabe would happily go along with our mothers' plan without complaint, but I never passed up an opportunity to earn brownie points with my mother in-law. "You can count on me, Mom." The brilliant smile I earned made me dance happily on the inside.

"You ladies have been gone all day. What else did you buy?"

"Um," my mom said hesitatingly. "We did some window shopping too."

I tipped my head to the side and studied her. While I was blessed with a poker face, my mother was not. The fact that she broke eye contact and began looking in her purse for something was a tell that she was hiding something from me. I really got suspicious when I saw Martina start to fidget too. I was about to press them, but the dads returned home and greeted their wives like they had just came home from war.

"I'm making dinner tonight," Martina announced to us.

"Yes!" I said, punching the air. "Can I help? I want you to teach me how to make authentic Latin food for Gabe. I'm sure he'd appreciate taco Tuesday if they were more like the kind you make and not the watered-down store version."

"I'd be honored."

When Gabe came home from work, he found me in the kitchen with Martina making tortillas from scratch.

"Oh my God," he said as he inhaled the aroma of the spicy shredded chicken and beef that we had already prepared. He came up behind me, wrapped his strong arms around me, and kissed a path from my collarbone to my ear. "You smell more delicious than the food."

Al called excitedly from the enclosed porch, and Martina went to see what he wanted. Gabe took that opportunity to pull up my sleeves and inspect my wrists. The marks had faded already since that morning.

"I got a little carried away," Gabe huskily said. "I love being physical with you, but I never intended to hurt you."

"You didn't hurt me, baby. I got a secret thrill every time I saw them today." I wanted to run my fingers through his hair, but they were coated in flour and cornmeal. My body often wore the marks of Gabe's passion; I loved each and every one of them. So, I told him so.

"I just wish I hadn't marked you somewhere that everyone could see it." Ah, we arrived at the real reason for his displeasure. He wanted to keep the magic we shared private between us. "I'll be more careful next time."

"When might that be?" I eagerly asked.

"I—"

"I'm back," Martina said. "Your father wanted me to see the snow flurries." Then she picked up right where she left off in her instructions. "I roll the tortillas out between layers of wax paper to make it easier and cleaner." I watched as she plopped the mixture on a piece of wax paper, covered it with another piece, and began rolling it in a circular pattern to get a perfectly round tortilla. "You don't want to work the dough too much because it will make it rubbery and chewy."

Gabe released me and stepped back so I could give it a go. It was as easy as it looked. "I'll never buy premade tortillas again," I announced. "What's next?"

"Now we fry them," Martina explained. "Cooking time depends on if you want soft tortillas for burritos, tacos, enchiladas, or chimichangas, or hard, crisp shells for tacos. Tonight, we'll make a variety so you get a feel for it."

"I can't wait," Gabe said, rubbing his hands together. "Are you planning on making the cinnamon crisps too?"

Martina pointed to the sugar and cinnamon mixture sitting in a bowl near the stove. "I can't believe you'd ask such a silly thing."

"Thanks, Mama." Gabe kissed his mother's cheek then went in search of our children.

"Big Daddy! Big Daddy!" Sassy and Savage squawked.

Martina and I worked effortlessly together as we prepared dinner. She was a patient teacher, and I was an eager student. By the time we finished, I was confident that I could whip up the feast on my own after she returned to Florida. I sat anxiously as I waited for Gabe to sample his favorite foods. My man loved food as much as I loved to feed him. It was almost a form of foreplay between us with his appreciative groans or grunts that would inevitably spill over into our bedroom later.

Midway through our meal, my mother put her fork down and looked at Martina, who gave her a quick nod. I knew we were about to learn what the two of them got up to that afternoon.

"Martina and I did some shopping today," my mother proudly announced.

"We think we found the perfect gift for the whole family," Martina added.

Al and my dad smiled at their wives, and I realized that they too were in on the surprise. I looked over at Gabe, and he shrugged indicating he was as clueless as I was.

"We decided to sell our homes in Florida and move here so we can be near our grandbabies," my mom announced.

"And our sons," my father added.

"Yeah, them too," Martina retorted.

Wow! Gabe and I just stared at one another for a few heartbeats. Gabe recovered from the shock first. "You're moving *here* full time? Do you mean you're moving in *here*?" He waved his hand around in the air to gesture our house. "*Here*, here?"

"We're not moving into your house, son," Al said. "We'd never impose on you like that. Your mother and Bertie simply mean that we're moving to Blissville."

"When did you decide this?" I was shocked, but certainly not unhappy about the development.

"During the two-day drive to get here," my father said. "Sure, we could fly, but lugging three months of clothes and cosmetics," he pinned my mom with a dark look, "is too much for a plane. Then there's the need to have transportation during our two-month stay, so driving was the only solution. We're getting too old for that crap."

"We talked about finding short-term rentals here, but that gets costly," Martina said. "Besides, two or three months a year isn't enough to see my grandbabies. You guys visit Florida when you can, which isn't often with such busy careers."

"This just felt like the right move for us," my father stated. "We want to be close by without being in the way."

"You're never in the way, Bill," Gabe assured him. "This sounds freaking awesome."

"I'm glad you approve because we toured some of the available homes at the new retirement community today and found two that we love a lot," my mom said.

"We can have the best of both worlds—time with our kids and grandbabies then return to our homes. That way no one's style is getting cramped," Al said.

"You're not cramping our style, Dad." The blush that creeped up Gabe's neck was adorable.

"Who said I was talking about you, boy? I need space to love your mama proper."

"Ew," Gabe said.

As if on cue, Savage began crooning his favorite Barry White song.

"That bird has uncanny timing," Martina said.

"And great taste in music," Al added, before he joined in.

If you can't beat them, join them. I snapped my fingers and sang along too. It was true though, I couldn't get enough of Gabe's love.

FIVE

Gabe

"YOU'RE AWFULLY QUIET THIS EVENING," JOSH SAID, JOINING ME in the shower. "Rough day at work, or is it the announcement our parents made?"

"Both, I guess." I pulled him toward me until his wet skin pressed against mine. "I'm not upset; I'm just processing." I slid my hands over the round swells of Josh's ass and gave them a hard squeeze, earning a pleased groan from my husband. "I have to be honest though, Sunshine. I don't want to talk about the parents while you're pressed against me naked and wet."

"Deal," he said.

I captured his lips in a fierce kiss that made my intentions clear. In case Josh needed a bigger hint of what I wanted, I slid a finger down between those firm globes, circled his tight, puckered hole, and raised it back up to the top of his crack where I teased the v-shaped indention there. Two years after our first kiss, I was still finding new parts of him to adore, to commit to memory.

Josh didn't believe in delayed gratification unless he was the one doing the teasing. He pushed his ass against my hand when my finger descended again. "Gabe." He half moaned, half whispered my name when I pushed slightly against his entrance on the second pass. Josh's cock twitched and pulsed as it slid along mine. Damn, I never tired of the way he made me feel with the simplest of touches or smallest sounds.

"Gabriel, you better fuck me like you mean it." Then there were his gritty demands that made it impossible for me to deny him, but that didn't mean I wouldn't prolong his torture just a little bit.

"All in good time, Sunshine."

I lowered myself to my knees in front of him. Josh's cock rose gloriously proud from his body, bobbing like it was greeting me. I darted my tongue out and teased the tip of it, capturing the excitement that leaked from his slit. He leaned against the glass like he didn't trust his legs to support him. A chuckle rumbled out of my throat because I loved having him at my mercy because the tables were usually turned since I was the one usually doing the begging and pleading.

Josh slid his hands in my hair and grabbed two handfuls when I licked a path from root to tip, circling the head of his dick, then trailed my tongue down to his sac. I sucked one of his nuts in my mouth then the other, because it's not right to play favorites. He widened his stance, encouraging me to go down on him further.

I lifted his tight balls and sucked the sensitive skin of his taint. I nestled my nose between his nuts as I left my mark on him.

"Baby."

Gone was his confident demand, and in its place, was a hoarse plea. He scored my scalp with his nails as I reduced him to one-syllable words and physical signals. Pride and power surged through me, spurring me to release him so I could start all over again.

"You're going to p-p-pay." His stuttered threat only made me hotter and hornier. Josh wanted my mouth fully on him, sucking him to the back of my throat. I thought about giving in, but where was the fun in that?

I met him halfway by sucking the head of his cock in my mouth and working that spot beneath the crown with my tongue that always drove him wild. Josh pushed his hips forward, trying to get deeper in my mouth so I pulled off him with an exaggerated, wet pop.

"Wicked bastard," Josh snarled. I loved it when he called me pet names.

I watched his abdominal muscles flex beneath his fair skin as the need to fuck, or be fucked, rolled through him. I had my husband right where I wanted him, but I wasn't ready to give in yet. I slowly worked his cock into my mouth until my lips were wrapped snuggly around the base. I breathed through my nose to work through the gag reflex then swallowed around the head of his dick.

My baby loved it when my throat massaged his cock, and I loved the pre-cum that dribbled down my throat in response. I continued working Josh to the edge then pulled off before he could fall over. I didn't think about the discomfort from kneeling on hard tile for so long, my only thought was outdoing any blow job I'd given Josh in the past. I wanted to burn that moment into his brain for eternity. He was mine. I owned every part of him down to the last drop of cum he shot down my throat when I finally let him climax.

Josh grabbed the bottle of lube then lowered himself to kneel in front of me. My cock pulsed and raged in his hand as he slickened it. Then he pushed my shoulders until I sat on my heels before he turned his body so that his back was to me. Straddling my thighs, he reached behind him to line my cock up to his entrance, and slammed down hard, spearing himself on my shaft. I grabbed his hips and held him still rather than let him ride me. Black spots dotted my vision as my cock throbbed and demanded release, but I didn't want it to end so soon. *Fuck!* Josh's chute tightened around my dick like an eager massage designed to give me the happiest of endings.

I turned my husband's head and kissed him hungrily as I fought to regain the control he took back from me with a few simple moves. My fingers twitched where they dug into his skin, trying to hold him to me, but they lost the battle when he began rocking his hips sensually. My grip went from holding him in place to bouncing him up and down my cock. The friction set flames licking along my spine and zapped my balls. My nuts retracted against my body seconds before I shoved Josh to his knees in front of me and pounded his ass, riding out my orgasm and busting my load inside him.

Afterward, I sat on my ass and held him on my lap as my dick softened inside him. "I can never get enough of you; I can never get close enough to you, Sunshine."

"Good," Josh smugly replied. "That means I'm doing something right."

"You do everything right, Josh."

"Not always," he countered. "I should've told you about Trent joining our pediatrician's practice. I risked giving you the wrong impression for the reason I remained silent."

I teased the back of his ear with my nose. "Talking about your ex-lover while my dick is still inside you is as bad as talking about our parents." I placed my hand over his chest where his heart still pounded from the excitement I gave him. "I didn't doubt your intentions, Sunshine. Besides, your heart is all mine so that putz can stay as long as he wants."

Josh eased himself off my dick and turned to face me. "I'm glad to hear you say that because I'm pretty sure I have to utter three words that pain me." The grimace that followed his confession made me nervous.

"What three words?"

"I was wrong."

I could quickly rattle off many times that I wanted Josh to say those words to me, but not in connection with his ex-boyfriend sticking around town.

"I heard that he's looking to buy a house." He said it so fast that it came out sounding like one, long word.

"For who? Him?" Jealousy and possessiveness clawed at my guts. "Are you toying with me right now?"

Josh's eyes widened in alarm then narrowed in irritation. "Have you ever known me to play games with you?" Josh's cheeks flushed a rosy red when I raised my eyebrow in response to his question. "I wasn't playing games with you then, Gabriel. I was terrified of you and all the delicious feelings you brought out in me. I have never lied or deliberately misled you," he clarified. "Mere told me today and now I'm telling you."

I released a frustrated breath then ran my hands through his hair. I didn't like that loser living in our town one bit, but it didn't matter because I knew that Josh had entrusted his heart with me. I wouldn't ruin that over something that was out of his control. "I trust you, Josh."

Josh set his pencil and sketchpad on the coffee table and reached for his hot chocolate.

He curled up beside me on the sofa in the sitting area of our bedroom suite. It was my favorite room in our house because it was a retreat for just the two of us. A fire crackled in the fireplace as I watched ESPN on the flat screen television mounted above the mantel. I couldn't tell you a thing I had watched, because I basically just looked at the television as my mind processed the revelations from that evening.

"Don't you want our parents to move here? You're acting kind of weird about it. You smiled like you were happy, but then you got quiet. That's usually not a good sign."

"Of course, I want them here. I want our children to really know them and not just see them a few times a year," I replied. "I just don't want them to regret it. My parents have only lived in Miami, Josh. It's one thing to visit here and enjoy the pretty flurries, but it's an entirely different animal to navigate through it day after day. People retire to Florida, not the other way around."

"Our parents aren't the kind of people who do things they don't want to do," Josh wisely said. "It might seem like they just decided it on a whim on the trip here, but I know better. This has been brewing since Destiny and Dylan took their first breaths. They were just waiting to spring it on us."

I snorted. "Yeah, probably so."

"We're going to need to set some boundaries, I think."

"You do?" I asked in surprise. "Like visitation times?"

"No, Gabe," Josh said like I was a dunce. "I can see our moms deciding that they want to be the ones to watch the twins while we work. They're going to tell us we can save the money we pay our nanny and put it toward the kids' college funds. And while that sounds amazing, it blurs their roles in the kids' lives. They're supposed to be grandparents who spoil them rotten, not the person that fights them to eat their peas and take their naps. Jennifer does an amazing job of that."

"Man, I bet she's enjoying her paid break though."

"Not really," Josh said with a smirk. "She texted me five times before noon asking about them. She's coming by to play with them tomorrow because she misses them so much."

"They are the cutest kids in the world." I tipped my head and thought about the point he raised. "Let's not borrow trouble, but we should have a response prepared *if* it's suggested."

"I think we need to keep Jennifer as their nanny, but let the grandparents take them out to do fun stuff when they want to."

"Which will be every day," I told Josh. "I think we're going to need to set some more specific parameters, Sunshine."

"I don't want to be too tough either, especially since they're moving here to be with them."

"That's their decision, not ours. We must do what's best for our family dynamic, and as much as I love our parents, under foot every day isn't where I want them. So, how do we do this?" I asked. "We don't want to be dicks and tell them how it's going to be, but I don't want them moving here under false pretenses either."

"Well, they haven't sold their homes yet, so let's put this conversation off until after Thanksgiving. The last thing I want is tension in the air while I'm preparing my feast. It'll make my turkey dry or something."

"I hate dry turkey," I grumbled.

"Right, so let's not ruin the happy vibes with wild assumptions on our part."

"Deal," I agreed. "What else happened today beside learning that Dr. Dickhead *and* our parents want to move to Blissville?"

Josh snorted. "I'm such a bad influence on you." I knew he was referencing the nickname I gave to *Trent.* "Doesn't have quite the same ring as the Dr. Dimples tag name that Chaz gave Kyle, but it's just as accurate." Josh got quiet for a second then a goofy smile spread slowly across his face. "I think Meredith is pregnant."

I sat up straighter and looked at him. "Think or know?"

"Think," Josh answered. "She was drinking ginger ale instead of coffee this morning. Meredith never gives up her caffeine."

"Maybe she had her limit for the day before she came over," I suggested.

"Not Mere." Josh shook his head. "She drinks a cup of coffee per hour." Josh knew her far better than I did, so I couldn't dispute that.

"I'm surprised you didn't come right out and ask her," I observed.

"It was hard, but I figured she was keeping it to herself for a reason. Maybe she just wants to hold onto it a little longer, or maybe she's waiting to do something fun and cute. All I know is that I better not be reading about it on Facebook with everyone else. Chaz and I gave her away at her wedding, so we deserve advanced screening of whatever it is she's planning."

I laughed at his hoity expression. "I'm sure Mere and Harley will tell their closest friends before they post it on social media. Who does that, anyway?"

"Everyone," Josh responded. "You wouldn't know that since you don't have an account."

"I think social media is evil," I told my husband. "People hide behind computers to bully and demean others."

"True, but that's only a small part of it," Josh explained patiently. "There are also the times that millions of people rally in support of a cause or a person who needs bolstering. It's a great way to stay in touch with friends and family who've moved away or learn about your favorite actor's favorite restaurant. It's the most effective advertising tool for the salon. It's not all bad."

"Yeah, I was really thrilled with the hateful Twister messages you got from that homophobic asshat that didn't think gay men should be allowed to adopt kids after you announced we were expanding our family during one of your segments on Channel

Eleven. Getting called a pervert on social media was a lot of fun."

Josh threw his head back and roared with laughter.

"What's so funny?"

"It's called Twitter, Gabe."

"Whatever it's called," I groused. "It's dangerous."

After that incident, I made Josh swear he would be extremely cautious about the photos he shared of our house or kids. I didn't want some crazed lunatic threatening the safety of my family. It was too fucking easy for people to obtain things about you that was none of their fucking business. Were those motherfuckers who sold addresses and phone numbers for a few bucks going to step up and protect my family from zealots who thought I should die because I love another man? Fuck no! Keeping my family safe was my number one fucking job, so that meant no pictures of our children would ever be posted on social media or on his show. *Whoa!* Apparently, I had a lot of fucks to give.

Josh agreed, of course, because we had more than just ourselves to worry about. In fact, one of the reasons for my chest-thumping started to kick up a fuss in her crib. We sat there listening to the monitor for a minute to see if Destiny would go back to sleep, if not we would snatch her out of there before she woke Dylan up.

Destiny became more vocal, and I imagined she was starting to kick her legs, making her displeasure at being ignored known. Josh started to stand up, but I put my hand on his wrist when another voice came through the monitor.

"Hush there, sweet angel," Bertie said. I could tell that she had picked Destiny up because she had stopped crying. "You're going to be a diva just like your daddy, aren't you?"

Josh smiled proudly. "Damn straight! She's going to be strong and assertive; a real force to be reckoned with someday."

"Your mom can't hear you through the monitor."

"I believe that *I* was the one who had to convince *you* of that fact," Josh told me. It was true; I worried that the sounds of us making love would be blasted through the monitors that Josh strategically placed throughout the house. "Besides, I was warning the universe."

I pulled him tighter against my chest and kissed his smart mouth. It didn't take long for my body to heat up and crave him all over again. "I have a force you can reckon with, Sunshine."

Josh rubbed my erection through my sweatpants. "I can see that, Captain Obvious."

SIX

Josh

IT WAS A DAMN GOOD THING THAT I GAVE UP BEING A perfectionist—or at least stomped the piss out of those tendencies when they popped up. There was no room for that ridiculousness when preparing a meal to feed over twenty people. I remembered the good ole days where I used my grandmother's china and real silverware instead of the paper plates and plastic utensils I've resorted to using on big occasions. I missed the formality, but not washing the dishes afterward.

"Is there anything we can do to help you, Joshy?"

I looked over my shoulder and saw that my mom and Martina looked eager to help but unsure of their reception. I had everything under control because I ran my kitchen like a seasoned chef. I advance-prepped the fuck out of everything I could and choreographed the rest of my cooking so that everything was done at the same time. I was grateful I had insisted on that wall double oven when we remodeled the house. Gabe said it was overkill because I had a third oven with my stove, but he quickly learned how wrong he was. Two turkeys, one spiral cut ham, and enough side dishes to feed a battalion took careful planning, time, *and* three ovens. Of course, the suggestion came from a man who wanted to *fry* one of the turkeys. No, sir. Not for Thanksgiving.

Even though I didn't need help, I greatly appreciated their offer. "I could always use your company," I told them. I suspected they had ulterior motives for their timely visit, but I kept my thoughts to myself and let it play out.

It wasn't until Martina started slicing mushrooms for the risotto that she spoke up. Handling Gabe's nemesis—the only food he hates—probably spurred her to action. "Are you guys okay with us moving to Blissville? Be honest, son."

I glanced over at her as I continued to sweat the mixture of celery, carrots, and onion in herbed butter. Martina's posture was rigid and she looked like she was holding her breath.

"We're thrilled that you want to be near us," I replied. "It's the best present you could've given to our family, Mom."

Martina released a shaky breath and gave me a relieved smile. "Yet, I'm sensing a but here."

"There's always a but," my mom added. "Is there something that concerns you, love?"

Gabe and I decided not to discuss our concerns with them until after Thanksgiving because the last thing we wanted to do was ruin anyone's holiday. However, it seemed silly to say that we didn't have issues one day then turn around and tell the truth a few days later. I decided to ease them into it by utilizing the tact I'd cultivated from dealing with salon clients for almost a decade.

I took a deep breath and released it. *Here goes.* "The only concerns we have are that you'll give up everything to move here and regret it later, or you'll be upset when we tell you that we intend to keep Jennifer as our nanny." It was my turn to hold my breath while I waited for their reaction.

When it came, it wasn't anything that I expected. The moms burst into laughter, clutching each other like it was the funniest thing they had ever heard.

"Josh, we have no desire to raise your children for you," my mom said haughtily.

"That's not exactly what I said," I told her, sounding more than a little irked. "We just didn't want your feelings to get hurt."

"Honey, we'll find plenty to do," Martina said. "Heck, Al is already thinking about opening a body shop here. He made more friends in one day here than we made the first year we moved into our new neighborhood in Miami. This is going to be a great move for us."

"We can't stand the idea of missing another Halloween like we did this year. Sure, the kids didn't go trick-or-treating, but seeing your family dressed as characters from The Wizard of Oz in pictures isn't enough. Gabriel as the Tin Man and you as the Scarecrow was so cute, and little Dorothy and Cowardly Lion were just too precious for words." My mom smiled through the tears that formed in her eyes. "We want to spend more time with our sons and grandchildren, but that doesn't mean we want to be in your face every second of every day. We won't tell you how to raise your children, but we'll be on hand if Jennifer gets sick or needs some time off too. I promise you that it will be a wonderful thing for all of us."

Everything they said sounded almost too good to be true, but

I decided to accept it at face value and deal with problems if, or when, they arose rather than trying to micromanage every little detail and person in my world. I smiled and said, "That sounds perfect, and we're so excited that you'll be here for all of Destiny and Dylan's milestones."

"Oh my gosh," Martina said wistfully. "First day of preschool…"

"And kindergarten," my mom added. "Blink and that day will be here."

"You know it," Martina agreed. "Oh, and visits from the tooth fairy."

"Next thing you know, they'll be going to prom and graduating from high school."

Tears filled my eyes, because as fun as those sounded, it would happen too soon. I wasn't ready for them to go to school and lose their teeth. They looked at Gabe and me like we hung the moon and stars, but someday they would look at us and roll their eyes because we were the stupidest people on the planet. And I sure as hell wasn't ready for the day that some girl or boy broke their hearts.

"Oh, I'm sorry, Josh," my mom said. "I didn't mean to upset you."

I blinked and wiped the tears that slid down my face. "Why does time have to go by so fast?"

Gabe walked into the kitchen just then with both kids in his arms. Hand to the heavens, I must've emitted some kind of signal because my man always knew when to swoop in and make things better.

"Daddy!"

"Daddy!"

Gabe took in my wet, swollen eyes and looked suspiciously at the moms. "What happened in here?" he asked suspiciously.

"It was the onions," I said, wiping my hands on my apron and taking the babies from him. That would explain the wet eyes, but not the trembling lips I pressed to one forehead then the other.

"He just realized how fast this year has gone and got a little emotional," Martina told Gabe.

"All lies," I said, trying to sound tough. "It was the onions."

"I've never seen onions make you cry in the years that I've known you," Gabe said. He smiled wryly as he pulled the twins and me into a hug. "I get it, Sunshine. I want to stop the ride sometimes too."

"Or just slow it down a little. I'm not ready for them to lose teeth, go to school, think we're stupid, or get their hearts broken." My voice was muffled against his chest, but I could tell he heard every word because he tightened his arms around us like he could protect us from all those bad things.

"Let's just enjoy today because it's all that we have, Sunshine."

I nodded after I pulled back. "I'm going to let the moms finish making the stuffing while I get the twins ready for our guests."

"Get ready? They're already dressed," Gabe said, sounding perplexed.

"It's like you don't even know me sometimes." I kissed his cheek and headed upstairs to the nursery. I wasn't sure I would dress the kids up extravagantly for every holiday, but you better believe I would for their first holidays. We had memories to make and hold onto.

Mama Richmond made Destiny the cutest little turkey day outfit I ever saw. It was a brown onesie that had a bedazzled turkey in crystals on the front. She sewed on an orange and yellow tutu and made brown, orange, yellow, and white striped leggings. We topped the outfit off with a big yellow headband that looked so beautiful against her coal black hair. She blinked her big blue eyes at me and clapped her hands because my daughter was already a fashion guru before the age of one. I knew she'd have our friends and family eating out of the palm of her hand. I was also certain that she knew it too.

I set her in the crib and turned my attention to her brother who was eating his fist. The kid was like his papa, ready to tear into his food. Dylan's outfit wasn't as fancy as Destiny's but it was equally adorable with a turkey face embroidered on the front of the brown corduroy overalls and feathers on his cute little tushy. His little turtleneck was made of the same soft cotton material as Destiny's leggings. Dylan's brown eyes sparkled in mischief as he tried to wrestle away so that I couldn't redress him. Our boy was a nudist at heart.

Gabe and I had the cutest damn kids in the entire land, which was proved by the aahs and oohs when we returned downstairs. Gabe grinned from ear to ear when I set them down and they toddled toward him. "There's Papa's little gobblers."

"Gobble! Gobble!" Sassy squawked.

"Eat me!" Savage added.

Gabe's eyes rounded innocently. "I'm trying, Sunshine. I think it will be easier to apologize for our kids' foul language than it will be to change Savage's."

"Probably."

Buddy ran into the living room from the kitchen looking guilty as fuck. "What did you do?" I asked him, not that I expected him to answer. He just lowered his head in shame then hid behind the couch.

I hurried into the kitchen to see the damage, confident it couldn't be too bad because the meats and side dishes were in the ovens. The only thing left on the counter was... "Oh no." I covered my mouth with my hand.

"What?" Gabe said, rushing into the room. "Did he get a turkey?" He skidded to a halt when he saw the carnage on the floor and gasped. "Worse!" He sounded so miserable that I expected to see tears in his eyes. "Please tell me you have a backup pie saved someplace. Don't fail me, man!"

I shook my head in disgust as I looked at the overturned pie plate and the sticky mess it made. "Well, of course I made an extra one just for you, but now it's the only one I have."

"My house, my pie," Gabe said sternly. "They'll have to eat pumpkin pie or that pumpkin crunch crap you made."

"Pumpkin crunch cake, not crap," I corrected, looking at him in disbelief. "You really want to deprive our guests of apple pie?"

"Fuck yeah," Gabe said in a tone a person reserved for the word duh. "Call Deanna; I bet she has one of those frozen ones."

"How about I make you another one this weekend?" I countered. His response was a glower that Brenda Leigh Johnson used on the shadiest of suspects. Here's the thing; I can't deny Gabe anything. The right thing to do would've been for me to put my foot down and use the reserved pie for my guests, but I couldn't do it. "Fine, but you're telling everyone it was *your* dog who ruined their dessert."

"I have no problem with that. I have plenty of experience managing hostile crowds."

"Well, let's hope this won't require riot gear," I quipped.

Our guests started filing in not long after the apple pie incident. Destiny and Dylan lit up like little Christmas trees when the older kids showed up. They gave up trying to walk because they were too slow to keep up with the Dorchesters and Adrianna. They dropped to their butts then scrambled after the kids at a fast-paced crawl, squealing and giggling as they went.

Gabe followed me to the kitchen to grab some drinks for our guests while I checked on the progress of the food. Everything looked and smelled delicious. Gabe must've thought so too because he swatted my ass on his way back to the family room.

Chaz and Mere were the next to join me in the kitchen. I told them everything that happened since I last saw them on Tuesday, which was surprisingly a lot.

"So, you're not looking for a new doctor?" Chaz asked humorously.

"Or a new place to live?" Mere inquired.

"No to both," I said. "We're mature adults now."

"Uh huh," Chaz said. His grin told me he was enjoying my potential misery way too much. "We'll see what happens when the kids have their next doctor's appointment."

"Bet Gabe takes them by himself," Mere added.

"Nah," Chaz said, shaking his head. "He'll stand in the corner with his arms crossed over his chest looking as menacing as he can."

"Hand on the butt of his gun," Mere added. "It would make a lasting impression."

"You two are a couple of comedians," I told them, but I couldn't stop grinning at the image they created in my mind. I still hoped for the best outcome, which would be Trenton moving on from Blissville.

"Where's Dare?" Chaz asked. "I thought he said he was joining us today."

"He sent a text and said he would be a few minutes late because he needed to pick up his date," I told them.

"Date?" Mere and Chaz asked at the same time.

"Since when is he dating someone?" Chaz followed up.

"I thought he was too infatuated with Wren to even see anyone else. Wren left town for the weekend so we know it's not him," Mere added thoughtfully. "Who else could it be? Memphis is already here. Beefcake Andy?"

"Better not be," Chaz said with widened eyes. Kyle still didn't like Andy anywhere near his man.

"We're running out of eligible gay bachelors," Mere said.

"Wouldn't it be funny if his date was—"

"No!" I said, cutting Chaz off. "That would not be funny at all."

"Maybe not to you, but the rest of us would sure as hell enjoy the show," he fired back.

I looked to Meredith for help but she was too busy laughing. Luckily for them, I blew off his remark because I knew it was his writer's creative imagination at work. There was no way the universe was mean enough to play a trick like that on me, right? Of course not. Don't be silly.

"Maybe he and Wren finally decided to quit circling each other and Wren decided to stay in town after all," Chaz offered as an alternate theory.

"That would be much better," I replied, crossing my fingers and toes that it would be so. The two men were as opposite as night and day, but there was an undeniable spark when they were in the same room. In fact, I wanted it to be true so bad that I half convinced myself that Chaz was right. I imagined the two fellas deciding to quit fucking around and start… *fucking* around.

Dare still hadn't shown up by the time dinner was ready, so I figured he changed his mind or something came up. I set out all the food and desserts buffet style while Gabe refilled drinks. We had just sat down to say grace after loading our plates to maximum capacity when the front door opened.

"Sorry that I'm late," Dare apologized. "I had a bit of car trouble."

"Where's your date?" Chaz asked.

"Oh, he's outside taking a call. He said that he'll be right in." No sooner had the words left Dare's mouth, the front door opened again. The cold breeze that entered our house with the new arrival was nothing compared to the icy chill that worked its way down my spine.

I heard a deep, rumbling growl from beside me. I wished I could say it was Buddy making a fuss, but it was my husband. "What's *he* doing here?"

I squeezed Gabe's thigh beneath the table. "Baby, I had no idea."

"Get rid of him," he said between gritted teeth.

I wasn't sure how to do that without looking like a complete dick to my friends, family, and my employees who had joined us. I thought that making a big deal over his arrival was the worst thing I could do. Trent looked at me and smiled crookedly. Did he enjoy riling up my husband? Did he have a death wish? I saw Gabe lean in Jon's direction and worried that he was hiring a hit.

"Everyone, this is Trent," Dare said, gesturing his hand between Trent and the rest of us. He was completely unaware of the tension he had created with his guest, and I wanted to keep it that way.

Trent looked over the food on display and said, "Oh, damn. I was hoping you made that amazing apple pie for dessert, Josh." *Yep, the dumb fuck had a death wish.*

SEVEN

Gabe

I KNEW DAMN WELL THAT JOSH HADN'T BEEN A VIRGIN WHEN WE met, but neither was I. We each had lovers in our pasts and neither of us owed an apology for the choices we made before we knew the other existed. It wasn't rational to be so angry about the other guy's existence, but I was furious. I hated the idea of that fucking prick touching Josh or making him come, but I couldn't really pitch too much of a fit with my ex-boyfriend—the one I had moved to Blissville to be with—sitting at our dinner table with us.

But, there were two big differences between Kyle and Trent: Kyle was invited, and the gleam in Trent's eyes said he was there to start trouble. If it was trouble he wanted; then it was trouble he would get. But first…

"You made him *my* apple pie?" I asked Josh, whose face was almost devoid of color. "*My* apple pie?" Okay, so I was irrational and slightly insane. I felt the eyes of our guests jockeying back and forth between me and the newcomer.

"Baby, it wasn't *your* apple pie when I made it for him," Josh said calmly. On some level, I realized he was right, but I felt as if Trent had walked into my house and kicked me in the nuts. Trust me, a man takes exception to that!

I stood up from my chair, tossed my napkin on the table, and pointed to Dr. Dickhead. "You come with me."

"Gabe, please…" Josh's hand snagged my wrist before I could leave the table.

I looked down at his face and saw the silent plea in the hazel eyes I adored. I pulled his hand to my lips for a kiss. "I won't be long, Sunshine." I glanced back at the doctor who wasn't looking quite as smug as when he first walked through the door. "With me." I turned and headed toward the kitchen, knowing that he'd either willingly follow me or I'd drag him by the scruff of his fucking neck. I'll give him credit though; he didn't make me wait long.

"Do you realize whose house you're standing in, Trent? Can I call you Trent?"

"Uh, sure."

"I'm going to need you to be a little bit more specific," I said, sounding like I was interrogating him. Hey, the bad cop never went away; he bided his time until he was useful again. "Are you saying 'sure' that you know whose house this is or that I can call you Trent?"

"Both," he answered nervously.

It wasn't just my tone of voice; I used my entire body to

intimidate that little weasel. I stood tall with my back ramrod straight and my chest slightly pushed out. I could break him with my bare hands but hoped it wouldn't come to that. It was highly frowned upon for police captains to rough people up. I could almost hear Josh's snark comments about another IA investigation.

"Why are you here, Trent?"

"Dare invited me."

"I know that part, but why did you accept? Furthermore, why did you walk in with that smug look on your face?"

"I wasn't aware that I had a smug expression on my face, and I thought dinner at Josh's house sounded good. He's a phenomenal cook."

"I know damn well that my husband is amazing *everywhere*, so I don't need you to start ticking off his attributes."

I crossed my arms over my chest as I remembered the way Trent had hurt Josh in college by making him feel that he wasn't good enough to introduce to his friends and family as anything more than an acquaintance. I saw the admiring glances he aimed at Josh the night that we ran into him at the hospital when Sally Ann gave birth to Adrianna and again when he walked in as Dare's guest. I knew fucking well it was no coincidence that he chose Blissville for his pediatrics rotation. It was best he knew where things stood to save himself from looking like an ass.

"Your breakup with Josh wasn't amicable so why the hell did you think it was a good idea to come here? Better yet, how'd you meet Dare to get an invite?"

"Um, my breakup with Josh was a long time ago," Trent countered coolly. "It's obvious he's moved on and very happy, or maybe not, if you think dragging me in here and warning me away is warranted."

I took one step toward him and he took two steps back. His little spark of bravado fizzled out beneath the menacing look I aimed at him. "He's deliriously fucking happy," I groused, "but I'm not here to speak on his behalf. My *husband* can handle himself just fine. I want to be sure you're not taking advantage of Dare's kind heart."

"I met Dare when I went to Curl Up and Dye to schedule a haircut last week."

Josh didn't tell me that Trent had showed up at the salon. I thought we had cleared the air and there would be no more secrets or attempts to keep me from losing my shit, but apparently not. The very thought of Josh touching Trent's hair made me want to punch the doctor in the face. I knew it wouldn't have the same meaning as when Josh massaged my scalp or ran his fingers through my hair when we kissed or made love, but still. He wasn't getting my motherfucking pie, and he would need to find someone else to cut his stupid fucking hair.

"I stopped in to see Josh, but he wasn't there, so Dare scheduled me an appointment with some other guy named Robin." His words relieved the tightness in my chest.

"Wren."

"Excuse me?"

"Wrong bird, dumbass. His name is Wren."

"I'm not a dumbass," Trent argued defiantly.

"Your actions today don't back that up." I held up my hand to cut him off when he opened his mouth to speak. "I'm not going to make a bigger scene than I already have, so you're in luck. You can stay, eat our food, drink our beverages, and join in on the conversation with our friends and family because this year is special to all of us for one reason or another. Do not look at my husband like he's on the menu again. Don't assume he's the same guy you knew years ago, and don't insinuate that your shared past actually means you know him, because I promise that you don't know the first thing about Josh Roman-Wyatt. So, Trent, the question is: can you eat dinner with us and behave?"

"You kind of sound like Clint Eastwood," he replied with a

crooked smile. "Yeah, I'll be good."

"Welcome to our home," I said somewhat cordially. "Grab a plate and dig in."

I remained in the kitchen after Trent left because I knew that Josh was hovering by someplace close and would want to speak with me. I was prepared for him to lecture me about my behavior, but instead he pushed me back against the counter and ravaged my mouth.

"Oh my God! I shouldn't encourage your ridiculous behavior, but it's so fucking hot. It makes me want to drag you and your knuckles upstairs and show you just how much I belong to you."

"Okay," I said, wrapping my arms tightly around him. "I'll let you." I had never been so disappointed that there wasn't a hidden staircase that led to our bedroom.

"Gabe, one day you're going to realize that there's no other man on this earth that I'd rather give my body and my apple pie to more than you."

The comment about the pie made the ridiculous jealous feelings stir inside me again. I could tell by Josh's smile that he knew it too.

"Gabe, I was only eighteen years old when I dated Trent. I didn't have access to bourbon, so the pie he remembers *is not* the same pie that I make for you." He ran his hands through my hair, and I practically melted into a puddle on the kitchen floor.

"You're not cutting his hair either."

"What are you talking about?" Josh asked.

I repeated what Trent had said. Josh snorted when I got to the part where he butchered Wren's name.

"Let's go enjoy our first Thanksgiving dinner with our babies," Josh said softly. "The nonsense with Trent doesn't matter. I won't be cutting his hair, and he can't cause trouble if we don't let him."

"You're right," I told Josh, earning a shocked expression. "Hey, I admit when I'm wrong."

"Uh huh."

"It just happens so rarely that you can't remember, Sunshine."

All eyes were on us when we returned to the dining room—well, all except Trent's. He kept his eyes on his plate of food while Dare looked worried and dejected beside him. I smiled at Dare so he'd know the things that transpired between Trent and me were not his fault. If anything, Dare was another victim of Trent's narcissistic personality. Dare reminded me of a younger Josh, and I found it unlikely that Trent had a change of heart when it came to flamboyant men. *But you did*, the pesky voice in my head reminded me. *Shut the fuck up*, I shot back.

I felt terrible when I realized that our guests were waiting for us before they ate. Josh worked so hard to prepare the delicious meal, and it sat getting cold while I acted like a jackass. I reached for Josh and tugged him to me once more. "I'm sorry that I ruined your delicious dinner."

"You didn't ruin anything; you were just being you. Besides, how do you know it's delicious?"

"You made it," I said as a matter-of-fact. I looked around the room at our guests. "I'm sorry I kept you waiting." I received various looks in exchange. The knuckle draggers in the group understood where I was coming from, even if they didn't realize the extent of Trent's past with Josh. The rest of the adults were a little more level-headed and wore bemused expressions. I was happy that I didn't see disappointment on our mothers' faces. In fact, they looked almost proud of my assertiveness. My two favorite little faces smiled up at their papa like I did a great thing.

"Let's say grace so we can eat," Meredith said. We all joined hands and bowed our heads. "Heavenly Father, thank you for the bountiful blessings you've given each and every one of us. Thank you for the love you've brought into our lives, for it is the greatest gift of all time, and one that never stops giving. We ask for your continued blessings and guidance in our lives today and each new day that follows. Please help us to realize the beauty in the world so that hate will never dwell in our hearts. In Jesus's name, we pray."

"Amen," we collectively said.

Then all talking ceased as we dove into our food like half-starved animals. I reached beneath the table and squeezed Josh's knee to let him know how much I loved every bite I crammed into my mouth. By the second round, lips started to loosen up to include other activities like talking. No one was quite sure how to approach the topic that was on everyone's minds. Okay, all but one.

"How do you know my son?" Bertie asked Trent.

"We met at college," Trent said cordially.

"Oh? Josh never mentioned you," she replied. I couldn't have loved her more unless she pulled a gun out of her purse and shot the prick. Bertie was not a gun-toting mama, so that is one fantasy I knew wouldn't come true.

Trent blushed because Bertie's comment could've come across that Trent was so insignificant that Josh never mentioned him. I wanted that to be the case, but the truth was that Trent, following so closely after the horrible relationship with Billy I-Hate-Myself-For-Being-Gay Sampson, really did a number on Josh. It was like Josh had told me. Billy was ashamed of being gay, but Trent was ashamed of Josh. I might not be the most perfect man on the planet, but compared to those two dumb fucks, I was quite the catch.

"Well," Trent said sheepishly, "I didn't treat Josh very well, so it's not surprising that he didn't tell you about me." Trent darted a quick glance in my direction before he looked at Josh. "It's really my only regret in life." *Did he mean that losing Josh or mistreating him was his biggest regret?* "I'm sorry, Josh."

"Fucknugget! Fucknugget!" Savage squawked. The bird's timing was impeccable as always.

"Please excuse Gabe's bird. He has terrible manners," Josh told Trent. *Hey, at times like these, I'll gladly take responsibility for Savage's dirty mouth.*

"Dirty Bird!" I said, but my voice lacked admonishment. I was in awe of my feathered friend.

"Bite me!" came Savage's reply.

"Bad Bird!" Sassy squawked accusingly.

"Cockbadger!"

Trent's slack-jawed expression was priceless, but the outlandish behavior barely got a response out of the rest of our guests since they were so used to it.

Josh just shook his head and talked over the crazy birds. "Thank you, Trent, but as you can see, I'm very happy. You really shouldn't give it another thought."

Yeah, what my husband said, asshole.

"Thank you for being so forgiving." Trent then looked back at me and offered a wry, but non-threatening smile. "I hope to have a fraction of this kind of happiness someday." I decided I would take that as a compliment and not his plan to steal my man and kids.

There was quite a bit of grumbling about the missing apple pie, but there was enough pumpkin crap to go around. I had to admit, Josh's homemade cinnamon whipped cream made the stuff tolerable, but it would never replace the love in my heart for his boozy apple pie.

Trent and Dare left not long after they finished eating. Dare looked like a kicked puppy, which made me dislike Trent even more. I hated that Josh 2.0 got his hopes dashed by the doctor. Once they left, the mood resembled that of our normal gatherings and the shenanigans ensued. Barbs were traded between spouses, complaints about sports were lobbed like weapons, and Josh took all our money in poker.

It was a wonderful evening, but I admit to being happy when our guests started going home. I heard Dorchester tell his wife that I was hoping to get lucky, and while that was true, I had an apple pie to devour first. I ran to the kitchen when the last car pulled out, not caring how ridiculous I looked. By then, I had learned where Josh stashed the good stuff. I yanked open the cabinet doors so hard that I nearly ripped the hinges off. I found a folded note in the place where I expected to find my pie.

Gabriel,

Your pie is upstairs in our room along with the very special whipped topping I made to go with it. I will feed the pie to you naked on your lap AFTER we put our angels to sleep.

Love,

Your Sunshine

Having that mini fridge in our bedroom suite had sounded silly when Josh first mentioned it, but it was another example of his evil genius. I took the steps two at a time, both eager to tuck our kids into bed, and get to the good times that I knew would follow.

Josh had already wrangled Dylan into his pajamas, so I got our princess ready for bed. She looked up at me with so much love and joy that it took my breath away. It was my turn to read, so I picked up the thick illustrated book beside their bed and settled with Destiny in one glider while Josh held Dylan in the one beside me. I held the book out so Dylan could see the colorful pages while I told them all about Winnie's latest adventures.

They were fast asleep long before I finished the chapter, but I kept reading so that my voice followed them into their dreams. I didn't need the holiday to remind me to be thankful for Josh and our kids, but I couldn't deny that somedays were extra special. Love and pride welled so full inside my chest that it nearly hurt to breathe.

My blessings extended to the privacy of our suite where my husband pressed his naked body to mine and fed me the most delicious boozy apple pie topped with homemade whipped cream that had vanilla liqueur and a splash of cinnamon whisky in it.

"I have a surprise trip for the entire family tomorrow," I told Josh after both my stomach and dick were content.

"We're not singing Christmas carols, are we?"

"That's a damn good idea, but not what I had planned." I didn't wait for Josh to guess again. "We're all going to the tree farm to chop down our family Christmas tree. We get to ride in a sleigh and everything."

"Oh man. We're totally going to end up with a Clark Griswold kind of Christmas."

EIGHT

Josh

"Get back in bed," Gabe demanded sleepily. "There cannot possibly be a good enough deal worth getting out of bed at four o'clock in the morning."

I rolled out of bed before he could get his hands on me because he would make me late for shopping with our moms, Mere, and Chaz. "You'll be thanking me come Christmas morning," I said smugly as I made a dash toward our bathroom. "Go back to sleep. You're going to need the energy for the lumberjacking you'll be doing this afternoon." I still couldn't believe that Gabriel Roman-Wyatt wanted to pack us all into a sleigh and ride out in the frigid cold to cut down a frigging tree. *Where had this even come from?*

I smiled when I came back into our bedroom after a quick shower and found him sound asleep once again. I ran my hands through his silky hair and kissed his cheek before I left our room to meet our mothers in the kitchen.

"Come on, Josh, we're going to miss all the good stuff," my mom whined.

"Here's your coffee, sweetie," Martina said, handing my favorite travel mug to me. Martina wasn't as enthused as my mom about our early morning excursion into the crazed crowds.

"Did you see the Toys 'R' Us ad?" my mom asked. "There are so many things we want to buy for our angels."

"Mom," I calmly said as I led them to the garage where Duchess was parked. "Gabe and I don't want the holidays to be about presents and material things. We're all about the experiences." Once the words left my mouth, I realized that was why Gabe wanted to do the tree thing. I had to admit, it sounded old-fashioned and sweet.

"I understand and approve of the sentiment," my mom agreed.

"I'm so glad you understand." Gabe and I worried that they'd take it the wrong way.

"Of course, I understand, but don't expect me to listen," she said sassily.

"Mommm," I whined.

"Listen, as you so eloquently stated yesterday, you and Gabe are responsible for raising the little monsters. Our job as grandparents is to spoil them rotten."

I looked to Martina for help, but none was forthcoming. "I call dibs on that toddler train set," she called out as she climbed in the back seat of my SUV.

"Dang it," my mom said. "Okay, but I get to buy that Victorian dollhouse."

"Wait! They're too little for train sets and dollhouses yet," I told them. I appreciated their holiday enthusiasm, but what was the point of buying a house full of stuff the kids can't play with for years?

"Darling, these are age appropriate," my mother said patiently. "We're not idiots."

"I never said that, Mom."

"Not in so many words," she countered. "Have a little faith in us, honey. Martina and I did a wonderful job with our own kids." She wasn't wrong.

"Yes, Mother."

Mere and Chaz were ready to go when I swung by their homes. Chaz had a ginormous cup of coffee, and Mere had something that smelled like chamomile tea. I was convinced more than ever that Meredith and Harley were expecting their first child. She had never gone shopping without a large cup of coffee to spark her to life.

"I bet a fight breaks out over toasters or some stupid shit," Chaz said hopefully. He was only there to people watch. "If something exciting happens, I can add it to the last-minute revisions of my Christmas novella."

"What's this book about, honey?" Martina asked eagerly.

"A stubborn, sassy hairstylist who fights his attraction to his true love," Chaz replied.

"Does Wren know that you're writing a book about him?" I asked innocently.

Mere giggled in the middle of the back seat. "Good one, Jazz." I glanced up and caught her eye in the rearview mirror. She grinned from ear to ear, looking happier than I'd ever seen her—including her wedding day. I was looking forward to the moment when I could stop playing dumb and congratulate her.

"Wren is stoic and mysterious, not stubborn and sassy," Chaz replied. "My new character resembles a certain blond guy we all know and love."

"I'd make a terrible book character," I said, waving off the idea as ridiculous. "Besides, I know you're just yanking my chain."

"Am not," Chaz said. "I even have a working title for the first book."

"Really? And what would it be?"

"The Brazilian."

"As in wax?" Mere asked.

"Uh huh," Chaz said absently, and I knew he was mentally making book notes. "It's also the nationality of the dead guy our salon owner trips over in the alley behind his shop. I want each of the book titles to be a play on salon services."

"Oh! The second book can be called The Blow Job! It's what we jokingly call a blowout," Mere said to the moms.

"I'm not sure how well that title would go over," Chaz said.

"Are you kidding?" my mom asked. "It would be awesome. This series would be great with graphic covers."

"Blow Me, Baby!" Martina blurted out enthusiastically from her shotgun position, sounding a lot like my blue-feathered pet.

"Oh! I like that even better," Mere said. "It's suggestive without being crude."

"Curled Hard and Put Away Wet," my mom suggested.

"Oh man! These are great," Chaz told them.

I didn't have to look to know that he was making notes in his phone. I smiled as I merged into traffic with the rest of the insane people out and about before the sun was even up. I had a feeling it was going to be a day I never forgot.

"Excuse me, Officer. I do believe I'm entitled to a phone call." The cop just sneered as he slammed my cell door shut. *Fuck my life!*

"You've been watching too much television," he groused.

"No, it's because my husband is a police captain," I said firmly. It sounded better than reciting episodes of *The Closer*.

That got his attention. He turned, gave me a harsh once-over, then sneered. "Yeah, right," was all he said before he walked away.

"Blissville Police Department," I yelled, but wasn't sure if he heard me before he closed the door.

I flopped down on the hard bench then winced. *How the fuck did things escalate to the point that I was arrested?* My mom, that's how! Not that it was her fault, but it didn't matter, because Gabe was going to kill me. He'd especially be angry if we were late getting home and ruined his tree chopping excursion. I vacillated between wanting them to leave me there and calling Gabe to get me out of the slammer. I feared his reaction, even though I knew damn well that I was justified.

Apparently, the officer must've heard me and decided to look up the name of the BPD's captain and saw that our names did match because he came back not fifteen minutes later and released me on my own recognizance with a warning.

"You're lucky the lady didn't want to press charges," he told me.

"I'm lucky? You watch that video footage and tell me how lucky *I* am," I replied, shaking my head. "That lady was a psycho who physically attacked my mother, yet somehow *I* was the one who was arrested." The more I thought about it, the angrier I got, but I could see I was barking up the wrong tree with Officer Numb Nuts.

"Joshy!" My mom burst into tears when I walked out of the holding area. "Are you okay? Did they hurt you? I called Gabe and he took care of everything." There went my chance of burying this under the damn rug.

Lord, the only thing injured on me was my pride. "I'm fine, Mama. It's best we get on home, so I can face the music."

"I told Gabe everything that happened," my mother tearfully assured me. "He knows that your arrest was bullshit."

I appreciated my mom's optimistic outlook, but I knew my husband was most likely wearing out a hole in the carpet from pacing. He wouldn't look at my actions as justified, he would view them as potential for getting hurt. I reminded myself that fear would be at the heart of the blustery reception I could expect to receive.

"He wants you to call him," my mom added when we got in the SUV.

I wasn't dumb, I dialed him straight away.

"Do you have me on speakerphone, Josh?" he asked in a dangerously dark voice. See! Not dumb. He wouldn't blast me like he wanted to with everyone listening. He'd have an hour to calm down before we got home, longer if we stopped for lunch.

"Yes," I said, trying to sound calm. The truth was I was afraid, not of Gabe hurting me, but of seeing disappointment in his eyes. I was used to seeing love, respect, and adoration when he looked at me. Sure, I'd made him mad, or confused him plenty of times, but I never disappointed him. The fact that he used Josh instead of Sunshine was the biggest clue as to the trouble I was in. "I'm sorry, Gabe."

He released a long, frustrated sigh. "Just get home safe, Sunshine."

I released a sigh of relief. "I will." I disconnected the call and asked, "Who's hungry?"

"No way," Mere said. "We're going straight home."

"But, Mere."

"Can it," she firmly said. "You did nothing wrong and we're going to tell Gabriel so. It was complete bullshit what that woman did then cried foul when you called her out."

"I got it on video!" Martina exclaimed. "So help me God, I'll release this on You TV if they show a false portrayal on the news." I suspected that Martina was about as familiar with social media as her beloved son and meant YouTube, but I certainly wasn't about to correct her. I needed her on my side.

I groaned because I hadn't even thought about cell phone videos. Oh man. There'd be ten different edited versions floating around by the time I got home.

"It was a setup," Chaz said calmly. "We'll make sure Gabe listens and understands."

Too bad Gabe grabbed me by my Burberry scarf and practically dragged me up the steps to our bedroom without giving my fan club a chance to talk him down. "Are you okay?" he asked, but he sounded more pissed than concerned.

"My pride is hurt that I didn't see that setup for what it was," I replied. "Your mother has the entire video on her phone."

"Great, we can show it to Dylan and Destiny as part of your highlight reel, because I can guarantee there will be plenty more fits in the future," he said hotly.

I put my hands on my hips and aimed my best indignant expression his way. "And just what do you expect me to throw a fit about, Gabriel?" Apparently, he didn't notice my tone of voice or the way I skipped using his nickname.

"If Dylan doesn't make captain of the baseball team or Destiny doesn't make the cheer squad," Gabe said. "Oh, I bet you'd raise a fuss if you're not allowed to send birthday treats to school. I hear that they're cracking down on that stuff nowadays. No cupcakes and fruit punch, you get carrots and water." He kept rambling on, completely unaware that I was stewing.

"Maybe I get my knickers in a knot if *Dylan* doesn't make the cheer squad or Destiny doesn't make captain of her softball team," I corrected him. "It's a little early to be deciding their extracurricular activities, isn't it? I'd also like to think that as gay men we wouldn't guess their hobbies based on their gender either."

"Now, Sunshine, you're deliberately misunderstanding what I meant, so you can divert the attention away from yourself. That's not going to work this time," Gabe said, but I noticed he was quick to drop my cutesy name.

"Save it, Gabe. I'm not in the mood. I need to put on warmer clothes if we're going to traipse through the woods to find the perfect tree." I heard the deflation in my voice, and I was sure he did too, but did he understand why? I thought that disappointment was the worst thing I could see in his eyes, but I was wrong. Ridicule was far worse. He didn't give me a chance to explain anything, he assumed the worst, *and* mocked me. It felt a lot like the time we broke up two years ago. I knew we were in a much stronger place, but damn it still hurt. "Just give me a few minutes to myself please. The twins have new snowsuits in their closet."

"Sunshine…"

"We'll talk about this later."

I walked to our closet and willed him not to follow me. Thankfully, something went right for me that day because he honored my request and had the twins suited up by the time I joined our family.

I planted a fake-ass smile on my face, but I could tell that I wasn't fooling anyone. "Is everyone ready?"

We crammed ourselves into the minivan with all the enthusiasm of people attending a wake. I wanted to do or say something to lighten the mood, but you know what? Fuck it! Gabe wisely kept his mouth shut during the drive out to the tree farm, which was good because I was working myself into a good snit.

How dare he? Gabe was supposed to know me better than anyone, but he thought I actually hit that woman over a thirty-dollar plastic toy.

I wanted to hold onto that anger, but I had to admit that the atmosphere at the Christmas tree farm was majestic. The buildings looked like rustic log cabins you'd expect to see in the mountains. I saw a gift shop, a café where you could buy hot beverages and other goodies to eat on your excursion, and the stable where you boarded the sled. Each of the buildings were decorated with tasteful white Christmas lights. I guess I expected something cheesy like dancing snowmen or Santa inflatables instead of the Norman Rockwell experience it turned out to be.

"Mom, can you take the twins a minute, so I can talk to Josh?"

"Sure," both moms replied.

"I'm not sure I want to talk to you right now, Gabe," I said after he pulled me to the rear of the vehicle.

"I know that you don't, but I don't like this tension between us." Gabe breathed deeply, held it for a few heartbeats, then released it slowly. "I know damn well that you didn't hit some lady at the fucking toy store. I knew it before my mom snatched me by the shirt and made me watch that woman throw herself down and scream foul." He ran the back of his hand over my cheek before trailing his fingers over my lips. "I was just worried that you could've been hurt. You know I don't react well when your safety is in question."

"I know," I replied softly. I couldn't hold onto my hissy fit when he looked at me with his melted-chocolate eyes. Damn him. "What about the rest of it?"

"Sunshine, I will never be the father who stifles his children. If Dylan wants to be a cheerleader then I promise to be the best cheer dad on the planet. If Destiny wants to play softball, I'll teach her how to slide into home base. Tell me that you believe me."

"I do." I knew in my heart that Gabe was just using examples earlier and not trying to pigeonhole our kids into gender specific roles. "I'm sorry too. I should've been smarter."

"Hopefully, it will all blow over," Gabe said. "If not, my mom is ready to release her video on You TV." He rolled his eyes. "Even I know it's called YouTube."

"What else is bothering you?" I asked when I saw that our reconciliation only chipped away at his tension.

"Damn Christmas Bandits struck again."

"Bandits?" I questioned.

"They hit too many houses for it to be one person and not get caught."

"What happened this time?"

"They cut the wires for exterior lights and stole a bunch of lawn ornaments," Gabe replied. "I had hoped the incident at Santa's Village was going to be an isolated stupid prank, but it's not looking good."

"I'm sorry, babe. I know you're going to arrest these Christmas Bandits."

"We better get going if we're going to find a tree while there's still light," Al said, interrupting us.

"Be right there, Dad," Gabe replied. "But not before I do this." He gave me a quick kiss full of passion and promise. "Let's go find our perfect tree."

The sleigh ride was fun, the hot chocolate was delicious, and we found the most amazing tree for our family room. As nice as all of that was, my favorite part was when Gabe took off his coat to reveal a red-and-black-checked flannel shirt. He rolled up his sleeves and began chopping down the tree with the ax in smooth, steady swings. His big strong hands, and thick forearms made me shiver hard and sweat beneath the fur-lined flannel blanket.

I finally understood the hype about lumbersexuals, and I was going to show him my wood at my earliest opportunity.

NINE

Gabe

DAMN, WHOSE BRIGHT IDEA WAS IT TO CUT DOWN THE FUCKING tree and drag the fucker home? Oh, yeah. Mine. I was starting to get grumpy until I saw that familiar, but never old, gleam in Josh's eyes that told me something I was doing turned him on. I was so getting lucky, even though I'd acted like a jerk. Because I wanted to please my husband, I really gave him a show. I put everything I had into my swings and went full-out Paul Bunyan on that bitch.

"You might want to take it easy," my dad called out. "You don't want to throw your back out."

I scoffed of course because I was in the best shape of my… "Oh, fuck!" I dropped the ax to the ground, narrowly missing my toes on my right foot, when the mother of all spasms wracked my lower back. "Son of a bitch!"

"Gabe!" my mother admonished. "The children." She and Bertie placed their hands over Dylan and Destiny's ears, which were covered with both a thick, knit hat and the hood of their snowsuits. They were a scarf away from looking like Randy from *A Christmas Story*. Even if they did hear through the multiple layers, those kids had heard far worse from the birds.

"Hurts bad." *Damn me and all my showing off.*

Josh was there in a flash, his hands rubbing up and down my back. "Baby, what can I do?" I tried to stand up but another spasm wracked my body hard. It hurt so bad I thought I was going to puke.

"I have muscle relaxers at home, son," my dad said when he joined Josh and me. "I get spasms occasionally and they're the very devil. Add in a hot shower and you'll be just fine. Let me help you to the sleigh." My dad was the only one big enough to support my weight. I threw my arm around his neck and leaned into him while Josh walked ahead to move everyone around so I could sit in the front row. I was pissy that I was missing my chance to grope him beneath the blanket in the back row of the sleigh.

"We can't leave without the tree," I said between gritted teeth.

"I'll finish it," he said. "You could've had that thing cut in two by now if you weren't showing off for your man." His chuckle rumbled from his chest. "I swear to God, you're just like your old man. Flexing your muscles and carrying on."

"That obvious, huh?"

"Don't be embarrassed. It's natural to strut your stuff like a banty rooster. Let's make you as comfortable as we can, and I'll push the tree the rest of the way over. " His laughter echoed through the pines. I was glad he was having such a good laugh at my expense.

"Baby, I'm sorry," Josh said. At least my husband was sympathetic to my misery.

"Why are you apologizing?" I asked. "I'm probably the one who jinxed this outing with my dickish behavior before we left."

"You were just worried about me, Gabe. Sure, you could've handled it better, but I always know your blustering comes from a place of love."

"That doesn't make it o-o-ouch! Damn it!"

"Hurry, Al," Martina said. I expected my dad to already have the tree chopped down, but instead, he stood there posturing so my mom could get an eyeful. "Oh my!" she said.

"Ewwww," Josh and I said at the same time.

Of course, mine started out "ewww" but ended with an "owww."

Our sleigh driver, coincidentally named Nick, tried to get us back as fast as he could while jostling me as little as possible, but it was pure misery.

"Maybe we should take you to Urgent Care for X-rays," Josh suggested.

"Let me try taking one of my dad's muscle relaxers first," I told him, squeezing the hand he placed on my knee. I gasped as my muscles contracted and twitched painfully. "If that doesn't help then we'll go back out and leave the babies at home with our folks."

It sounded like a good idea, but Josh ended up driving us all straight to Urgent Care when the pain became too intolerable for me to take. It was the last way I wanted to spend a Friday evening with my family, but I worried that my dad's pills wouldn't be strong enough.

Luckily, they got me back in an exam room quick instead of making me wait. I was sure it pissed off the people who were there before me, but I wasn't there for a cough or sniffle. I was fucking dying and needed help, dammit. Josh and I left my parents in the waiting room with strict instructions to guard the babies from the icky germs floating around.

I saw a physician's assistant first who injected something amazing into my body. The relief was immediate as a drug-induced fog invaded my brain. "Sweet relieeeef," I slurred.

"The doctor will be in to see you in a minute," the physician's assistant said.

"S-s-sounds gooood." I tried giving him a thumbs-up, but my hand felt too heavy to lift. "Heeeey, babe, I wonder if *this* doctor has seen you nekkid too?"

Men with lesser egos would be horrified that I made them sound like a lab coat banger. Not my Josh. "It's not likely since the doctor on call is a woman," he replied.

"You've never seen any lady bits? You weren't curious at all if maybe you like the pussy too?" *Like the pussy too? Fuck, I was high.*

"Noooo," Josh said, "but clearly you did."

"I couldn't keep an erection and the poor girl was horrified. We both were," I amended.

"Um, hello. Mr. Roman-Wyatt?" a hesitant voice asked from the doorway. I hadn't even heard her knock because Josh was laughing too loud.

"I like cocks and I cannot lie."

"Okay, Savage," Josh said patiently. "You're going to be traumatized in the morning if you remember this conversation." Josh turned to the young doctor who stood looking back and forth between us. "Hello, I'm—"

"Josh Roman-Wyatt," she said, cutting him off. "I recognize you from Channel Eleven. I love your series." Then as if she remembered where we were, she extended her hand to Josh and then me. "I'm Doctor Tomlinson. What happened tonight, Mr. Roman-Wyatt?"

"I tried to be a sexy lumberjack, a lumber sensual, or whatever they call it."

"Lumbersexual, dear, and you pulled it off spectacularly until you threw your back out."

"I feel"—yawn—"much better"—yawn—"now."

"I can see that," Dr. Tomlinson said. "I'm going to write you a prescription for muscle relaxers. Would you like pain pills also?"

"No," I said adamantly. I hated taking anything stronger than Advil, but muscle relaxers were a must.

"Okay," Dr. Tomlinson said, "I'm going to recommend you see a chiropractor right away. If they're not able to help you, they'll refer you to an orthopedic doctor. Often, chiropractic care combined with massage therapy will correct the problem."

"My husband gives the best massages," I said dreamily. "He has magic hands."

"That should go a long way to help you feel better," Dr. Tomlinson said. I could tell she was doing her best to remain professional and not burst into laughter. "I hope your weekend gets better."

"Yeah, me too," I said to her. "Take me home, Sunshine. I'm ready to finish trimming the tree so we can decorate it."

"I think we'll have to save that for tomorrow," Josh replied, tucking close to my side and supporting my weight the best he could.

"I'm totally good to go all night long. You know that about me, Sunshine."

"Sure thing, tiger," Josh said. I could tell he was mocking me, but I would show him. I'd have the most perfectly trimmed tree in its stand in no time *and* rock his world. Probably all before dinner!

"Okay, I might need a little nap first."

Next thing I knew, I was waking up in our bed next to Josh. He was lounging on his back reading a book while wearing my flannel shirt that he left open to reveal a skimpy pair of black bikini briefs. I, on the other hand, was completely naked. My brain wasn't the only thing waking up either.

Josh turned his head and smiled at me. "Feel better? I got you in to see Dr. Minske in the morning. He'll crack you back into place."

"How'd you know I was awake? I didn't move or say anything."

"I could hear the blood rushing to your dick." As if to test his theory, he reached beneath the blanket and wrapped his hand around my dick. "Yep, I knew it."

"I'm alive, naked, and you're practically naked too. I'd be more concerned if I didn't have a hard-on. Come over here."

Josh tossed his book aside and rolled over into my open arms. "You didn't answer my question."

"I still feel a little groggy and there's a dull ache in my lower back, but thank fuck those evil spasms have subsided."

"Roll over onto your stomach. Let me see if I can do something about the dull ache."

I slid his hand down to my junk. "Baby, I guarantee you can cure all that ails me."

"We'll get to that after I try to work some of the kinks out of your back. Go on, roll over."

Like I would refuse my husband's hands on my body. I tucked my arms beneath my pillows and got comfortable while Josh straddled my thighs and rubbed oil into his hands. "That smells good. What is it?"

"It's a mixture of chamomile, marjoram, rosemary, and thyme. The chamomile helps reduce inflammation, the marjoram helps with aches, pains, and muscular cramping, rosemary helps ease the soreness, and thyme fights the fatigue in your body." Josh pressed his hands to my lower back then leaned forward to press his lips to my ear. "Close your eyes and relax, love."

Relax? How about melt into a puddle of goo on his fancy sheets. "Mmmmm." Josh expertly dug his thumbs into my back with the perfect amount of pressure. He worked the tight muscles to loosen them up then expanded out and up until the only thing not relaxed was my cock.

"How's that feel?" he asked.

"Hurts," I whined.

"Still? Where?"

I lightly bucked my legs and Josh moved his knees, allowing me to have a little more freedom. I spread my legs wider, giving him a view of my cock and balls. "Make it better."

Josh reached his slick hands between my legs and pulled my sac with firm, delicious pressure. "You like that?"

"You know I do."

He continued to massage my sac with one hand while teasing my crack with the other. My pucker pulsed with anticipation when Josh circled it with a finger, but instead of pushing in like I wanted, he went back to trailing his finger from my taint to the top of my crack.

"Stop being mean; I'm injured."

"I'm not being mean; I'm drawing out your pleasure." Josh removed his hands from my body and I heard him open the cap to his oil bottle. I closed my eyes and imagined him drizzling the oil over his fingers to coat them well. My eyes jerked open when Josh drizzled the oil along my crack instead.

"I want to feel you inside me. That's what will make me feel better."

Josh drew out my torture slash pleasure by leisurely stretching me open for what seemed like eternity. "You'll have to tell me if this gets uncomfortable." He pulled his fingers out of my ass, and I felt the pressure of his cock at my entrance. With one quick thrust, he pushed in all the way to his root.

"Mmmmmm," was all I could manage. I loved the burn of penetration and knowing that Josh was as close to me as a person could get. It had been a while since he'd fucked me, and I needed a minute to adjust. Josh remained still until my breathing evened out then he moved like only he could. Slow, smooth and as naturally as when he danced for me. His hips circled and he stroked in and out, in and out, driving me out of my mind.

"You feel so good, Gabe. I'm about to embarrass myself."

"Never," I mumbled into my pillow. I loved knowing my body brought him so much pleasure. There had been times that I came before him, but I still took care of him. Just as I knew he would do the same for me.

Josh's hips snapped forward faster as he chased his orgasm and it was my name on his lips when he spilled inside me. "God, I need to do that more often." I grinned at his love-drunk confession.

Josh surprised me by rolling me to my back. I wanted him to spear himself on my cock, but he didn't want to put pressure on my back. Instead, he fisted my slick cock and jacked me. His hooded eyes stayed locked on mine while he worked my cock until my body trembled hard and I came all over my stomach and his hand.

"C'mere," I said groggily.

"Let me go get a warm washcloth for you," Josh said, trying to avoid my grasp.

"A little oil never hurt someone." My eyelids felt like one of those dolls my cousin Sheila had. When you laid the doll down, its eyes automatically close. Sit the doll up, her creepy eyes opened. No matter how we tried, we could never get the doll to do the opposite of what it was designed to do. No amount of prying was going to keep my lids open either.

Josh let out a resigned sigh. I heard the lamp click off and felt the bed shift as he cuddled up next to me. The warmth of his body acted as another catalyst to lull me to sleep, sort of like pouring gasoline on a fire.

"What's on your to-do list tomorrow, Clark?" he asked smartly. It took my sluggish brain a minute to figure out who Clark was. He was referring to the movie *Christmas Vacation*.

"Rigging up the lights."

"Christ."

"Well, it is his season," I smartly said just before sleep claimed me.

TEN

Josh

I CRAZY LOVED MY JOB, THAT WAS NEVER IN DOUBT, BUT I couldn't remember a time when I was happier to get back to work than the Tuesday after my Thanksgiving break. Hell, I had been tempted to go in on Monday to see if any walk-ins stopped by.

"Wow, your dad and Gabe did a fantastic job on the Christmas lights here and at your house," Mere said when she arrived at the salon. Like usual, we were the first to show up.

My father decorated my childhood home every year as far

back as I could recall, and I didn't realize how much I missed his handiwork until I took over the duty. Of course, I decorated the salon for all major holidays and the four seasons, but I never had my dad's knack for outdoor lighting. Luckily, he taught Gabe, who we all know has the patience of a saint. Gabe recovered quickly after his trip to the chiropractor and was a fast learner, which was the reason he could handle me so easily. In fact, he was usually one or two steps ahead of me. It took some time for me to get used to it, because I liked being in control and always know what lay in wait around the next corner.

Learning to trust Gabe, allowed me to love him. Loving him gave me the confidence to let go of my ironclad control and have faith in him—us. I still occasionally fell back on my old routines when yoga, jogging, a spin on my pole, or Gabe's, wasn't enough to quash the anxiety building inside me. After the weekend I had, you could say that my anxiety was high alert level.

Mere sat on the floor beside me in the stockroom. "You okay, baby?"

"I will be, Mere. How about you? Are you feeling okay?" I blamed the excitement of the holiday, our parents' big announcement, my arrest, and Gabe's injury for the reason it took me so long to realize why she was keeping her news a secret. She was scared out of her mind. She'd once told me that Mama Richmond had several miscarriages before she delivered Mere and a few more afterward when she tried giving Mere a little brother or sister. When I had that aha moment at four o'clock in the morning, it took everything I had not to call her. Her need for sleep was the thing that finally stopped me from dialing her number.

"So far, so good." It was the closest thing to a confession as I would get out of her, but that was okay. I didn't need to hear the words.

I laced our fingers together and lifted her hand to my mouth for a kiss. "I bought you some whole milk. I read that it's good for you." I couldn't get back to sleep, so I read an article on what expectant moms need the first trimester. It had been a while since Meredith complained about "shark week" with other women on the staff or clients, but I was pretty sure she hadn't hit that twelfth week mark yet.

"Thank you so much." Meredith burst into grateful tears like I'd presented her with the hope diamond.

"Anything for you. We're going to get through this together like we do everything."

"I love you," she said through sniffles.

"I love you too."

In the old days, Chaz would be the one to find us hanging out in the stockroom, but he was at home creating fictional worlds. I sure hoped he was joking about creating a series about a hair stylist. Who the hell would read that? Dare was the one who found us leaning against one another. My arm was around Mere's shoulder and her head was pressed against my chest. Dare might have been a newer employee, but he knew my habits well.

"Am I the reason you're freaking out?" he asked me, his eyes pleading with me not to be angry. As if.

"Not even close," I told him. "Besides, the situation with Trent wasn't your fault."

"Who's Trent?" a deep voice asked just out of sight.

Dare's eyes rounded in surprise before he schooled his features into a neutral mask and looked over his shoulder. "It's no one for you to worry about, Wren."

I didn't have to see Wren's face to know he was giving Dare his patented squinty-eyed glare. I expected to hear the music from *High Noon* playing as the two men squared off. It was funny to me that Dare was the only one who didn't see how he tied Wren up in knots. I'm not talking a pretty little bow either, I'm talking a knot so complicated it would take months, if not longer, to untangle.

"Why don't you let me be the judge of that," Wren returned

with a bite in his voice. "Was it that *doctor* who stopped in here last week to see you?" Oh yeah, he wanted to do some biting all right.

"He was here to book an appointment for a haircut last week, not see me." I heard the eyeroll in Dare's voice and wished I could see his face. I also wished for some popcorn.

"Who'd you schedule him with?" Wren wanted to know.

Oh shit! Please don't tell him...

"You," Dare said sassily.

"Well, won't that be fun?"

I jumped to my feet then. I couldn't allow my salon to become a casualty to their stupidity. "Guys—"

"You wouldn't dare—"

"Oh, I dare to do a lot of things—"

"Guys!" They had no intention of listening to me. I held out my hand and helped Meredith off the cold, hard floor.

"Like what, Wren?"

"Plenty of things," Wren said stubbornly, but I could tell he was running out of steam. "None of them are your business." *Oh, but he wants them to be.*

Of course, Dare didn't say what he was really thinking or feeling either. He went with, "You're such an asshole, Wren."

"Yes, I am. It's best you remember it too."

"Like you'd let me forget it," Dare dramatically replied before he stomped out of the little room.

Wren poked his head around the corner. The expression in his dark eyes could only be described as defeat. "Sorry, boss."

"It's not a problem. Don't worry about Trent, I'll—"

"I'll cut the fucker's hair," Mere said, interrupting me. Then she looked at me and waved her finger back and forth. "Remember your promise to Gabe." I wasn't sure that Mere would be any kinder to Trent, but he at least had a fighting chance with her.

"Thanks," Wren said, smiling wryly. "I owe you one."

"Was I this clueless when it came to Gabe?" I asked Mere once we were alone.

She giggled and poked my rib with her finger. "Worse."

Nothing filled my shop to capacity quicker than murder or mayhem. The visitors that day wanted to chat about my arrest. I was horrified when a video of me arguing with that woman went viral, but glad it showed me in the best light possible. She was the one who looked like a complete nutter throwing herself to the ground and yelling like I had pushed her down.

"Josh, I loved the way you defended your mama from that evil woman," Mrs. Handerneski said. She was the first client in my chair that morning and she spent three hundred dollars on salon gift certificates. "The perfect stocking stuffer."

"Thank you, ma'am."

"Your hair stayed perfectly styled the entire time you played tug of war over that toy," Mrs. Randolph said while I put foils in her hair. "It was amazing." Of course, I had to show her what held up so well during my brawl over a talking, dancing, stuffed bear. I might've gotten thrown in jail, but my mama came away with that motherfucking toy.

"I'll take two," she told me.

Gabe stopped by with lunch, and I knew he was still trying to atone for the weekend. It wasn't his fault that I was arrested, and had the situation been reversed I might've freaked out a little too. Yeah, he got a little overzealous with the ax at the tree farm, but we still ended up with a beautiful tree and I got me some lumbersexual sexy times after he felt better. I shivered because I was pretty sure I had finger marks on my ass from him gripping me so hard. Not to mention that our home and business looked amazingly festive.

So, yeah, our crowded house and hectic weekend had me feeling out of sync, but that wasn't his burden to shoulder. Realizing that, was the bucket of ice water I needed to get over myself. "Hey, you wanna sneak into the mixing room like old times?"

"It's occupied," Gabe said with a smug smile and a playful wink. "I think Wren is finally done fighting his feelings for Dare."

I thought back to the back and forth sniping that morning. "I don't think so, Gabe." No sooner had the words left my mouth, a dazed and stunned Dare stumbled out the door and walked in a trance-like state back to man his desk at the front of the salon. "That doesn't mean anything."

Wren came out of the room next looking like he couldn't believe what had happened. He briefly touched his hand to his mouth and watched Dare's sassy walk. Wren's eyes met mine and his face turned a bright shade of red.

"Been there, done that," I told him, hoping to ease his embarrassment.

"Excuse me. I just need a minute," Wren mumbled then walked out the back door, presumably to get some air and gather his wits. He looked turned on and a little angry too.

Gabe and I turned our attention back to the reception area. Dare sat in his chair staring off into space looking bewildered as fuck. I wondered if he was even aware that he was tracing his lips with two fingers or if his hand moved on its own.

"Been there, done that," Gabe said, nodding at Dare. "Must be something the stylists drink in here that helps them drive a man to the brink."

"Oh, I thought you were referring to the wonderment Dare appears to be experiencing," I replied, trying my best to sound like I had hurt feelings.

"Baby, you're the king of wonderment, but in the beginning, you were equal parts pleasure and pain. Maybe even sixty forty with pain taking the slight edge."

"But you're not sorry."

"You are the best thing to ever happen to me, Sunshine. Never doubt it for a minute."

My chest swelled with love and tenderness for the world's sexiest police captain. Oh, that reminded me. "On a scale of one to ten, how bad were you harassed this morning over my arrest on Friday?"

"Thirty." *Shit!* Gabe crooked his finger for me to lean toward him. "Don't you worry about it; I can handle myself."

"Hey, the mixing room is free now." I waggled my brows suggestively.

Things clipped along at a happy, drama-free pace until about three in the afternoon. It started when Mere got sick. She assured me it was normal and swore she was good to go, but I sent her home to rest. She looked more relieved than angry when I walked her to her car and made her promise to call me later. Wren and one other stylist had lighter schedules that afternoon and offered to pick up her clients if they didn't want to reschedule. Dare started making calls and I wasn't surprised to hear which clients were flexible and which ones wanted to wait for Mere to return. Of course, Mere offered to stay later through the week to make up for it. I was happy that most of the clients were willing to work with another stylist rather than have Mere working twelve-hour days.

I thought the crisis was diverted until Dare received a bouquet of flowers from a delivery man. I knew by the look on Wren's face that he didn't send I Want to Fuck You flowers, which meant they were an apology from Trent. I was familiar with his moves, in fact, I think it was the same type of mixed flowers he sent to me all those years ago. Wren stared daggers at the colorful blossoms while Dare gushed over their beauty. I was pretty certain he planned to sever the flower heads with his shears as soon as he got the opportunity. I bet he would pretend they were Trent's head too while laughing maniacally. *Damn, I'd been hanging around Chaz and his overactive imagination too much!*

Eventually, Wren stopped glaring at an oblivious Dare and things fell back into a peaceful rhythm. That all came to a screeching halt when Trent showed up for his haircut around five. Fuck! I never asked which day he was scheduled. Mere went home, Wren looked like he was going to stab Trent in the eye at any minute, the other chairs were all filled, which left only me to cut his hair. I promised Gabe though. I chewed on my bottom lip for a few seconds before I made an executive decision. I was a laidback employer, but I could put my foot down when it was needed.

"Wren, can I please talk to you for a minute?"

"Sure," he said, but he hadn't budged from staring at Trent and Dare.

"Wren," I repeated. The second time got his attention and he followed me to the kitchenette. "I need you to cut Trent's hair and preferably without piercing his nut sac with your shears."

"Damn, I hadn't thought of that. Thanks, Josh."

I shook my head in frustration. I clearly wasn't getting my point across if he thought I was trying to help him ruin my business. "Listen, I can't cut his hair or my husband will hunt him down and kill him. I need you to put your difference aside and cut the fucker's hair." Wren's mouth dropped at my salty language. "Furthermore, get your head out of your ass and you won't have to worry about some jackass creeping in on your guy."

Wren was a big guy—tall and strong, but I went toe to toe with him. There was no way that I was letting Trent leave my salon unsatisfied so he could complain to people. He was just the type too. There would be no letter to the editor about my salon. Fuck no!

"Yeah, okay," Wren said after a long pause. I liked that he didn't dispute that Dare was his guy. "But I don't have to like it."

"Certainly not," I agreed. "Go out there and show Dare that you're a mature adult. After we close, ask him to go to dinner with you."

Wren scoffed like it was the dumbest thing he ever heard. I leveled him with the look I gave to my husband when he was being too stubborn to live.

"I'm sorry if you thought I was joking. I've been watching the two of you circle each other like pissed-off alley cats for too long!" That last part came out louder than I planned it. "Knock it off, and get each other off, Wren. We'll all be better off for it." Okay, that was totally inappropriate, but he seemed to like that remark.

"Yeah, okay."

"Atta boy," I said, placing my hands on his broad shoulders and turning him. I gave him a gentle, but firm, shove. "Go get him."

I was congratulating myself when I returned to the salon, but my relief was short-lived when I overheard Trent confirm dinner plans with Dare. I took one look at Wren's face and made a hasty decision that I hoped I wouldn't regret.

"Wren, you have an important phone call," I said, lying through my teeth. "I'll cut Trent's hair." I held up my shears and smiled wickedly at Trent. "Right this way," I said gesturing to my chair. "I'll be right back."

I went into the kitchen and sent Gabe a quick text.

Baby, Mere went home sick and Wren wants to kill Trent. I have to do it. I promise it won't mean anything to me. It's just business. Love you, bye.

Then I turned my phone off, slid it in my pocket, and hoped for the best.

ELEVEN

Gabe

I DIDN'T DRIVE ACROSS TOWN TO THE SALON TO SUPERVISE THE haircut like I wanted to, especially after Josh turned off his phone after sending the text. Of course, I wasn't surprised when my call went straight to voicemail. He had made his decision then went about his business. Josh had never once manipulated me by purposefully triggering the possessive beast that lived inside me. He was confident in my love for him and wasn't starved for attention. I teased him about being a diva, but he was easy to understand once you peeled back the layers and got to the heart of the man.

His love for his—our—salon was a close second to his love for his family and friends. I could tell from his text that he felt stuck between a rock and a hard place. I even chuckled a little at his attempt at humor. It was true that I had nothing to worry about, so instead of making a fool of myself and embarrassing my husband, I remained home and waited patiently for him to come home. Okay, I wasn't the least bit patient and frustration probably rolled off me in waves as I paced the floor of his dance studio. I assured my raging beast that Josh belonged to us, but he needed more than words; he needed a demonstration.

That's why I sent Josh a text to let him know where he could find me when he got home and provided an acceptable way he could atone for breaking his promise to me. I wasn't mad, just annoyed. It seemed like that damn Trent somehow orchestrated everything to go his way. I didn't like it, or him. I didn't want my husband's hands on any part of his body.

"Are you going to make me dance for my supper?"

I was so preoccupied that I didn't hear Josh walk into his studio. I rounded to face him. I hated the apprehension and worry I saw in his warm eyes. I wasn't out to punish Josh; I wanted to connect with him in a way that only we shared. "Something like that," I said, offering a crooked smile to lighten the mood.

"Gabe, I—"

Closing the gap between us, I cut off his words by taking his mouth in a rough, hungry kiss, capturing his gasp and tasting his surprise. I was always so hungry for him, so fucking hungry. It never went away nor did it lessen. It grew with every beat of my heart.

"I haven't worked on a routine in a long time," Josh said sheepishly when we pulled apart to breathe.

"Yesterday, I heard a song on the radio and it transported me up to this room."

"Transported?" I could tell that it took a lot of control for him not to snort.

"That's what you do to me, Sunshine. I hear a song and see you dancing on your pole." I placed my hand on his neck then leaned my forehead against his. "I want you to strip down and dance for me, baby."

I took my seat in the padded chair in front of his pole and watched as he slowly removed his clothes, swaying to a rhythm only he could hear. When he stood in front of his pole wearing nothing but his pair of navy-blue briefs, I hit play on my phone. A shiver worked through me when "Believer" began to play, because Josh made me a believer in all things.

"Nice choice."

He said nothing else after that, choosing to communicate through spinning and dancing. Josh let the music work through him as he alternated between sensuous moves on the ground or spellbinding moves on the pole that showed off his flexibility and agility. I knew it took a lot of strength for him to look like he was walking on air. I loved watching the ripple and play of muscles beneath his beautiful skin. My eyes locked on his round ass, knowing I would soon part those cheeks and sink my dick deep inside him while he cried out my name.

I didn't recall the song being so long the first time I heard it, but maybe it was my eagerness to get at him that made it seem longer. I wasn't complaining though because I asked for my man to dance for me, and he didn't disappoint. I removed my clothes and coated my cock with lube in anticipation of the moment I could feel his bare skin against mine then crossed the room and captured him in my arms as soon as the last note ended. I yanked his briefs down his legs so that he stood naked in front of me.

Josh wrapped his legs around my waist when I lifted him and raised his arms above his head to grip the pole. "You gotta love a man who comes prepared to fuck." Josh hungrily licked his lips and said, "So, fuck me already." He undulated his hips, grinding his ass against my raging hard-on and his dick against my abs.

He didn't have to tell me twice. I slid one hand between Josh's parted legs to work his ass open while he devoured my mouth like he might not get another chance. Damn, my man knew how to turn me inside out and make my body beg for more. My blood pulsed through my veins, especially along my shaft, making it throb deliciously. The urge to fuck him was greater than my need to breathe, but I didn't want my pleasure to end too soon.

"Fuck me, Gabe!" Josh demanded, riding my fingers. "I want you inside me now."

He was as desperate to have me as I was him. Knowing that he was right there on the beautiful edge of sexual sanity with me made it that much sweeter, hotter. My need was ignored so I could focus all my attention on him, and my man loved having his ass played with. I alternated between teasing strokes with one finger where I barely grazed his prostate to pegging the gland with two fingers. Then I pulled out and circled his nerve-laden pucker to ratchet up his desire even more.

"I've learned my lesson," Josh said between gasps of pleasure slash pain from getting so close to his climax before I brought him back down. The desperate way his body shook made both my heads swell.

My reason for demanding a dance from my husband was more out of selfishness than one of life's teaching moments, but maybe subconsciously I did want to show him that he belonged to me. I lined my dick up to his ass and penetrated him to the base of my cock in one hard push. "All mine," I growled against his throat.

Josh squirmed on my cock like a worm on a fishhook, but not from discomfort. He wanted me to move inside him. I saw how much he wanted to take control. *Not tonight, my love.* Suddenly, it was a battle of wills like old times—both of us pushing the other to the limit; neither of us willing to budge. My husband got his way nine times out of ten, but that was one night I refused to give in.

I kept Josh pressed tight between my body and his pole, ensuring that he didn't have the mobility to work my cock like he wanted to. I knew what he liked, knew what he needed, and set out to show him who was boss, if only for a few minutes. Josh yanked my hair when the combination of the push-pull friction of my cock inside his ass and the drag of his cock against my abs drove him to the edge.

I kept my eyes locked on him as I gritted my teeth and fucked him with everything I had. The Josh I first met would've closed his eyes or tried to block me from seeing the love and joy my body gave him, but not the Josh I married. He smiled wickedly because he knew it was only a matter of time before he turned the tables on me, and I would enjoy every fucking second of it.

Josh took a few staggering breaths before his mouth fell open and he came on a silent scream like a sexy mime. His chute tightened almost painfully around my cock, tearing my orgasm out of me. When the last quake faded, I stumbled to the chair with a boneless Josh still draped around my body.

"Don't drop me, Captain Caveman!"

"Oh, that's my new favorite!"

"Your caveman routine is hot as fuck, but I never try to bring that out in you on purpose." Josh smoothed back the sweaty strands of hair that were plastered to my forehead. "Surely you know there is no one else for me."

"I do, Sunshine, just as I know that you don't make me insane on purpose." Josh quirked his brow. "Poor word choice. You don't deliberately poke the beast. It just happens naturally when it comes to you."

"And I reap the benefits," he said smugly. "Sorry I got home so late, but everything went sideways after lunch." I raised my hands and began rubbing his shoulders to ease the tension from them.

"Mmmmm. That feels so good."

"Why don't you go take a hot bath while I reheat the vegetable soup my mom made and fix you a grilled cheese to go with it."

"The only thing better than a hot bath is one with my even hotter husband," Josh said. "I'll come downstairs and keep you company while you fix my dinner."

"Don't you mean supervise me?"

"Come now, Gabriel. I'm not that bad." He laughed at the look of disbelief I gave him. "Okay, maybe a little."

***

"Mmmmm, you're getting really good at this," Josh groaned.

"I've been practicing. You like?"

"Oh, baby. It's the best you've given me yet." He licked his lips before he took another bite.

"I came down for peanut butter and jelly on toast and a glass of milk, but maybe now isn't a good time," my dad said from the doorway.

"Have no fear, Dad," Josh said, "I'm complimenting Gabe on his improved cooking skills."

"All right, I'll just go about my business then."

I leaned closer and lowered my voice. "I think all of my skills have improved since I met you."

Josh turned his head and slowly closed the distance between us while staring into my eyes and smiling like a man in love. My heart swelled with pride that I put that look on his face. Just as our lips touched, my cell phone rang on the table. The caller ID showed it was Adrian, and I knew it wasn't good news if he was calling me instead of spending time with his family.

"I think we have a problem, Captain," Adrian said gruffly. I heard scuffling in the background followed my shouting. "Shit!

You were supposed to secure the detainee, Officer Anderson."

I immediately went on high alert. "What's going on, Adrian?"

"Damn rookie made a huge mistake that could've cost us our lives. Luckily, our suspect was only interested in escape and Anderson was a state champion sprinter."

"I'll be right there. Where are you?" I asked.

"The alley behind Books and Brew," Adrian replied.

"I'll be right there."

"What's wrong?" Josh asked once I disconnected the call.

"Adrian said they've made an important arrest—one that Barney Fife nearly blew."

Josh snickered at Officer Anderson's nickname. "Be safe," he said then tilted his head up for a kiss.

"I'll be home as soon as possible, but don't wait up for me. The twins fell asleep early tonight so that means they'll be up with the roosters. It's your turn to get up with them."

"I smell a conspiracy," Josh said suspiciously. Between the two of us, he was the morning person. I grunted and used one-word replies until my second cup of coffee.

"I love you, Sunshine." I dropped one more kiss on his pouty lips before I went upstairs to retrieve my gun from the safe in our bedroom. My dad was waiting for me at the bottom of the stairs when I came back down.

"Be safe," he said, echoing Josh's words. "I love you, son."

"I love you too, Dad," I said, hugging him tight. "I'll see you in the morning."

I bent down and looked through the window at the prisoner in Anderson's squad car. "Is this some kind of joke?" I asked Adrian. I stood back up and looked at my former partner. "Who is this kid?"

"This *kid* was caught red-handed trying to break into the back door of Books and Brew," Adrian said. "No ID and refuses to talk."

"Runs fast," Anderson grumbled.

"Seriously?"

I know what you're thinking. Aren't you the guy who was taken down by the seventy-year-old woman? Yes, that was me, but this kid couldn't have been more than eleven years old. This was no Christmas Bandit or hardcore criminal. There was no way that he was sophisticated enough to pull off those burglaries on his own. Could he be part of a ring?

I bent down and looked into the window again. That time, the kid turned, and our eyes met. The sadness I saw in his expression punched me in the gut, robbing me of my breath. Maybe I wasn't the greatest judge of character all the time, but my track record was pretty impressive. "This kid isn't our criminal mastermind."

"I agree with you on that," Adrian said.

I stood up and motioned for Adrian to follow me a few feet away so that the boy wouldn't overhear us. "Do you recognize him?"

Adrian shook his head. "I know almost every person who lives in this town, and I've never seen this kid before tonight. He could live in a neighboring community, but judging by the condition of his clothes and his hygiene, I'm guessing he's a runaway. He's not wearing a coat or gloves and it's twenty-five degrees outside. The dumpsters were open behind the business and there are signs that someone went through them. They would not have found much since trash pick-up was this morning. I think the kid tried to break into Books and Brew to find food."

"He won't tell you his name or anything?" I asked.

"Hasn't said a word," Adrian replied.

"Take him back to the station, fingerprint him to see if we can find a match in the juvenile system, enter his height, hair, and eye color into the databases for missing kids to see if we can find a match. Oh, and call children services. I'll meet you there in a few."

"Where are you going?" Adrian asked as I walked away.

"The diner to get him something to eat. Maybe he'll be willing to talk with a full stomach."

The kid reminded me of a wounded, half-starved animal. He looked at the food suspiciously, wanting to refuse it, but the will to survive wouldn't allow him to pass up the opportunity to fill his belly. He ate with his fingers, getting food everywhere, while Adrian and I watched through the two-way mirror. Adrian's assessment about his hygiene and clothes were spot on. How long had this kid been hiding among us and why didn't any of us see him?

"Found a positive match for our would-be criminal," Officer Anderson said as he entered the room. "Marissa Smith from Goodville."

"Marissa?" Adrian and I both asked.

It was impossible to see the kid's features through the dirt and grime, but the buzz haircut and clothes made me think we were dealing with a boy. "Are you sure?"

"She has a juvenile record, Captain. Her caseworker, Susan Musgrave, will be here any minute."

Susan Musgrave looked relieved to see Marissa, but also a little worried. "What did she do?"

"She tried breaking into a local business," Adrian told her. "We think she was looking for food."

"Why did no one in Goodville let us know that a kid from our county was missing? Why wasn't her picture all over the news?" I demanded to know.

"Her foster parents didn't report her missing to us or the

Goodville police," Susan said furiously. "I assure you that there will be hell to pay over this."

Susan pushed open the door to the interview room and we followed her inside.

"Marissa, are you okay?" Susan asked softly.

"Don't call me that, Susan," the child tearfully replied. "My name is Mark. Why won't anyone call me that?"

I waited for Susan to correct the child, but instead she reached across the table and covered his hands. "I'm sorry, Mark. Can you tell us what happened to make you run away from your foster home?"

I suspected I knew, but I listened as Mark began to talk about his most recent heartbreaking experience at his latest foster home. It boiled down to a family who refused to accept that Mark was a transgender boy. The arguments started a year ago and escalated to the point where he no longer felt safe living there, so he ran away to Blissville.

"We're not going to pursue charges," I told Susan once we stepped outside the interview room to talk.

She looked at her watch and said, "Normally, I'd be thrilled, but I don't know what to do with Mark tonight. I can try placing him with another foster family, or in a group home. I don't want to keep putting him with people who won't accept him as he is."

The world could be a cruel fucking place for transgender kids, but I had a feeling that this particular kid made the right decision when he ran toward my town.

"I know just the couple. Let me make a call."

TWELVE

Josh

"On the fourth day of Christmas, my true love gave to me, a beautiful transgender preteen," I sang softly so only Chaz heard me. "It's your first Christmas as a daddy. Awww."

I wasn't sure he was listening to a word I said as he watched Mark and Kyle decorate sugar cookies along with the rest of the kids and their parents in our ever-expanding family. Chaz and I baked them and the rest of the gang decorated the ones that made it to the table. I was a perfectionist and Chaz was a cookie monster, so I would guess that maybe nine out of every dozen that we pulled from the oven made it to the table. Cookiepalooza was one of our new traditions and a real crowd pleaser.

"Just when I'm convinced the world can't get any shittier, I only have to think about Mark trying to survive in the cold and eating out of dumpsters." Chaz shook his head like he was trying to shake himself out of a bad dream. "They didn't even report him missing, Josh."

I looped my arm around my friend's shoulders and leaned into him like I'd been doing for as long as I could remember. "He doesn't look like the same boy who showed up here with you guys for dinner two weeks ago. He was sullen and terrified of being rejected once again, but look at him now, Chaz." I gestured to the boy who held Adrianna's cookie for her so she could squirt icing on it while laughing at Jon and Emory's shenanigans. They promised to keep their cookie decorating PG-13, but I was having my doubts. "Look how he glows, smiles, and laughs in just fourteen short days because of the love and acceptance you and Kyle have shown him."

"He has nightmares," Chaz whispered. "His psychiatrist said it's normal after the trauma he's experienced, but I hate that for him. It just kills us."

"You can't change his past, Chaz. You're doing everything you can to help him cope with what he's been through the past few years while helping him transition into a bright future. The sky will be the limit for Mark." I kissed Chaz's cheek and gave him an extra tight squeeze. "Did I ever tell you how proud I am to call you my friend?"

"For being a decent human?" He tried waving off my compliment, but I saw him tear up.

"For being a remarkable man," I corrected. "When you guys went through your foster parenting classes, I know y'all were thinking babies and toddlers. Surprise!"

Chaz laughed as a few tears escaped and slid down his face. "Surprise is right. We thought we were going to take one more vacation before we started the adoption process."

"Hey, that sounds familiar."

I looked over to where Gabe sat between Destiny and Dylan's high chairs. He had red, green, and white icing smeared all over his face, his hands, and his clothes, but he'd never looked more beautiful to me. Gabe snatched a cookie off both of their high chairs and took a large bite out of them. Dylan belly-laughed like babies do, but his sister wasn't amused.

Destiny banged her balled-fists on her high chair. "Papa! Papa!"

"That's my diva!" I said.

Meow. I looked over to where my pretty kitty sat in the tall window in the family room watching the world go by, tail switching in irritation because she couldn't chase the winter birds or didn't like me sharing her name with anyone else. I thought it was quite possible that Diva was either plotting to kill me in my sleep or take over the world, but I couldn't be sure.

Turning my attention back to Chaz, I said, "We surely didn't plan on those two angels so soon, but I wouldn't trade them for all the vacations in the world."

"I'm not sorry," Chaz said with a sappy smile.

"Mark will make a great big brother someday too. Look how great he is with little kids." I nodded my head to where he had switched his assistance to the Dorchesters' two youngest kids.

"I've only been a dad for a few weeks and you're already expanding my family."

"*Someday,*" I reiterated. "Does that mean you've postponed your anniversary trip?" Kyle and Chaz's one-year anniversary was coming up on New Year's Eve.

"No, but we're changing things up a bit." Chaz lowered his voice and said, "We're going to take Mark to Disney World for

New Year's Eve. They will have a magical firework display to ring in the new year."

"That sounds like a lot of fun."

"It's one of Mark's Christmas presents, so please don't say anything."

"Your secret is safe with me," I assured him.

"When is your appointment for Gabe's surprise?"

"Tomorrow."

"Are you nervous at all?" Chaz questioned.

"Nah, how bad could it be?"

"This is going to sting a little," Vanessa, owner of Dream Ink Tattoos and Piercings told me. "This is a very intricate design you created, but it's beautiful."

"Thank you," I replied proudly.

"Ready? I might want to get even with you a little for all the waxing you've done for me over the years."

"Please remember that I'm not the one to wax your lady bits," I said, pleading for mercy.

"Fair enough," Vanessa said with a smile. "Here we go!"

Sting a little? Try like fifteen thousand needle jabs per five seconds or something crazy. It took me by surprise at first, but I got used to the vibration and sting of the needle.

After about an hour, Vanessa shut off the machine and looked over her work. "Outline is done. Let's take a little break and then I'll do the shading. What do you think so far?"

"I think it's amazing, Vanessa," I said, not able to look away from the whimsical family tree she inked into my skin. Mine and Gabe's initials were carved into a branch at the top of the tree, and our babies' initials and birth dates appeared in dangling apples on branches below. The tree was spaced out beautifully so additional apples could be added later if we expanded our family. The roots of the tree looked like veins that formed a heart, giving it the appearance of our family tree growing out of the heart. Under the tree, I wanted a powerful message in beautiful script. I chose: Love Makes A Family.

Gabe had never said how he felt about tattoos one way or another, but I had a feeling he'd love this one. I hoped he did, because it was here to stay. It took Vanessa another hour or longer to work shading of various grays to give the tree a lifelike appearance. I expected to see the veins of the heart pulsing on my skin.

I couldn't wait to show it off to Gabe and was glad I got home before him so that I could plan my surprise. Of course, it would have to wait until two kids and two sets of grandparents went to bed. I could show him sooner, but I suspected we'd be upstairs for a long while afterwards and Gabe hated the thought of his parents knowing what we were doing, which was hilarious because our parents weren't at all shy. I knew damn well they weren't always taking afternoon naps, so why couldn't we get away with it.

They'll be moving into their own homes soon. They'll be moving into their own homes soon. I repeated it over and over while I got dinner started.

"Who's ready for the Christmas parade?" Gabe asked when he walked through the door. Destiny and Dylan had no clue what they were excited about, but that didn't stop them from clapping their hands and reaching for their papa.

Gabe kissed the munchkins then made a beeline for the little monsters' daddy. Gabe's hello kisses were so much better than goodbye kisses. He stopped just short of me and narrowed his eyes. "Something is different about you." There's no way he could know that and Vanessa's tattoo parlor wasn't in Blissville, so no one reported seeing my dadmobile parked there. Okay, maybe having some ink made me feel a little different, but surely it wasn't enough for him to sense that like a bloodhound.

"Just kiss me, Gabe."

"Okay, but then I'm going to have fun exploring your body. Those clothes aren't new, so it's something else."

"The Christmas spirit is oozing out of my pores," I proclaimed.

"I'll make your spirit ooze later." Gabe grimaced when the words left his mouth. Then he schooled his features into what he called his Josh face, which isn't a compliment unless you like people thinking you look like a prim and proper spinster with a broom handle shoved up her ass. "We don't do cheesy in this house, Gabriel," he said mockingly. He dramatically batted his eyelashes, which was *nothing* like me, but somehow adorable and ridiculous at the same time.

"I think 'oozing' falls into the gross category, not cheesy," I corrected. "I don't imagine Chaz uses that phrase in literature. Oh my God! This one time we read a book that had an engorged, oozing penis in it and we were ill for days." I laughed hard remembering the text exchange we had after reading it.

"That's about as bad as describing a vagina as moist," my mom said when she entered the kitchen.

"Ewww," Gabe and I said.

"See?" she asked, patting me on the chest. "What's for dinner?" She didn't notice the way I winced, but Gabe sure did. "Isn't that funny? We have role reversal now, son. I walk into your kitchen and immediately want to know what's for dinner just like you used to do growing up." Mom lifted the lid off the pot simmering on the stove. "Mmmmm, spaghetti and meatballs." She finally realized that neither Gabe nor I had responded to her chitchat and looked at us.

"Mom, do you mind keeping an eye on the sauce for a minute?" Gabe asked calmly. "I need to speak to my Sunshine privately for just a minute."

"I better turn this down some more because I've seen how

long 'just a minute' is to both of you. Is there anything I can help you with?" We both looked at her with raised brows. "In the kitchen," she clarified then pointed toward the ceiling, indicating the second floor of our home where the bedrooms were located. "I assume you have things figured out up there." Her laughter followed us up the staircase.

"Are you hurt?" Gabe asked once we were alone.

"No."

"Take off your shirt."

"Oh, are you going to make me dance for you again. Hey, do you want to reenact that movie *True Lies*? You can be Arnold, and I'll be Jamie Lee." I was nervous, so I rambled, which only spiked Gabe's curiosity more. I honestly wanted to do something sexy like a little striptease to reveal my new badass ink.

Gabe wasn't on board with that. He crossed to me and lifted my shirt without warning. Gabe inhaled sharply then said my name on a slow sigh. "Baby, what did you do?" I had watched his face closely and saw the awe spread across his features. The worry lines around his eyes and mouth softened and smoothed out as he traced his finger over the tattoo. He didn't seem to mind that it was covered in ointment. "Does it hurt?"

"It's a little tender," I admitted. "It's an early gift."

"It's beautiful, Sunshine. It looks delicate and strong at the same time."

"That was the goal of the design. Individually, our lives are fragile and delicate, but when you connect with your soulmate, you form something intricately stronger that continues to grow and sustains life."

"You drew this?" Gabe asked in awe.

"I sure did."

"I want one too," he said. "Right over my heart like yours."

"I was kind of hoping you'd say that. Part two of your surprise is that I made you an appointment for tomorrow."

"I can't wait." Gabe rubbed his hands together gleefully. "First, Dylan and Destiny have their first Christmas parade." A smile slowly stretched across his face. "What are you dressing them as?"

"What makes you think I'm dressing them up? It's cold outside so no one would be able to see their cutesy little outfits, *if* I picked some out."

"I know you better than I know myself. You have something adorable planned for pictures for the parade. So, what is it?"

"Knitted reindeer sweaters that are lined with faux fur and hats with little antlers sewn at the top. I planned on painting their little noses red like *Rudolph*."

"That comes on tonight! Don't let me forget to record it."

I patted Gabe's chest. "I already took care of it when you made that crazy master list."

"Yeah, well my favorite comes on Friday night."

"*Die Hard* is not a Christmas movie, Gabe."

"Sure, it is," he argued. "It's the best Christmas movie ever. Shit gets blown up, terrorists get killed, and Badass Bruce saves the day. You don't get any more Christmas-y than that."

"Did you take that quote straight from his fan club?" I questioned as I put my shirt back on.

"What movie is a better Christmas movie than *Die Hard*?"

"Where do I begin?" I rolled my eyes dramatically. "*It's a Wonderful Life, Home Alone...*"

"Which *Home Alone*?" Gabe asked seriously.

"The first one, of course, even though the second one was good too."

"I think *Home Alone* is a close second to *Die Hard*," Gabe admitted. "You know, we could create a holiday movie of our own?" He waggled his brows suggestively. "A fun title *comes* immediately to mind."

"And that would be?"

"It's a Wonderful Hard-On starring Captain Cock and Jizzy

Josh." Gabe looked so proud of his suggestion.

"I… can't with you right now," I said once I stopped laughing. "That's one video we won't be filming this year."

"What happened to that oozing Christmas spirit from earlier?"

"Not on film, baby."

"Okay, fine."

"What about *Christmas Vacation*?" I asked my husband, pulling us back to safer topics. "You're one rogue squirrel and a crazy sled ride away from bringing that movie to life. Are you waiting on a bonus so you can buy us a swimming pool? Which one of our friends is cousin Eddie? It's Dorchester!" I realized that Gabe stopped sparring with me. "That expression is new, Gabe. What does it mean?"

"What expression?"

I wasn't falling for his dumb act. I replayed everything I said up to the part where he stopped talking. "Oh my God! We're getting a swimming pool!" I knew I had guessed right when he glared at me. I bounced up and down, mentally planning all the fun swim trunks I could wear, or skinny dipping with him in the moonlight after the babies fell asleep. "We're going to need a privacy fence."

"Already included in the budget." I saw the heat in his eyes and knew his mind had gone to the same place as mine.

"My surprise seems kind of small compared to yours."

"No way, Sunshine. This," he gently placed his hand over my heart, "is the sweetest thing anyone has ever done for me. I can't help but notice that there's room for more little apples on that tree."

"Just in case."

"I love the way you think." Gabe pulled me to him for a kiss that kept us upstairs longer than we planned, proving that my mother was right, as usual.

THIRTEEN

Gabe

"You never said anything about us being *in* the parade," Josh said between gritted teeth as he held Destiny's little wrist in his hand, helping her wave back at the crowd. The twins were a big hit with their cute little sweaters and hats.

"Did I forget to mention that? The officers wanted to have a float this year, and I thought it was a great idea."

"Don't play dumb with me, Gabe. If I'd known you were going to literally parade me all over town, I would've fixed my hair or put on a hat to cover up the mess you made of it."

Complaining wasn't the type of sound that vibrated along my dick when I had fisted my hands in Josh's hair. No, he moaned and urged me to fuck his face. He loved a little roughness, and I gave it to him. Of course, I couldn't call him out on it, and his wicked smile said that he knew it.

"Smile at Grandma!" I said, pointing to where my mom stood beside my dad, Bertie, and Bill on the sidewalk filming the procession. "Wave for the camera!"

"I'm going to get even with you," Josh managed to say around a smile.

"Looking forward to it, Sunshine." I loved his brand of justice.

Blissville might've been a small town, but we sure knew how to celebrate the holidays. The streets were lined with people who came to hear the marching band play their Christmas favorites, see Santa throw candy out of an ornate sleigh that was pulled by horses instead of reindeer, and the floats built by the local businesses. My favorite float was Books and Brew's *'Twas the Night Before Christmas*, but Edson and Emma's diner was a close second since they did *A Christmas Story* theme complete with a giant leg lamp. Kyle's Santa Paws float was pretty damn cute too, and I was happy to see Mark smiling shyly on the float with Chaz, Kyle, and the staff from the animal hospital.

I was surprised that Curl Up and Dye hadn't entered a float, but Josh had chosen a different way to advertise each year. He sponsored the hot chocolate and popcorn so that his salon logo appeared on the Styrofoam cups and popcorn bags in a festive silver and gold font Josh only used for Christmas. He also donated salon packages that the village commerce council raffled off to raise money for their next community event. His salon packages typically raised over five thousand dollars, which would go toward the Fourth of July fireworks.

"Y'all need a better theme for your float next year," Josh said once we reached the end of the parade route.

"I said they wanted a float, not that they had great ideas," I whispered in his ear. I snapped my fingers and pointed at him when an idea occurred to me.

Josh looked at me warily. "Watch that thing; it could go off."

"You like it when that happens," I quipped then hooked my free arm around his shoulders to pull him and Destiny tight against me and Dylan. "I have an idea."

"Famous last words," Kyle said as he approached. "Don't fall for it, Josh."

"Oh, I know this well." Josh stopped and rounded on me. "No, I'm not designing a float for you next year. If I wanted to whip the town's ass with an amazing float, I'd do it for Curl Up and Dye. You need to plan this better next year, darling."

"Oh, next year I'm going to bring it," I said boldly.

"Is this a cheer competition?" Chaz asked, but neither Josh nor I acknowledged him since we were locked in a standoff.

"I would wipe these streets with you, Gabriel." Josh gestured up and down the street flamboyantly.

"Challenge accepted, Joshua." I stared into my husband's eyes without blinking.

"This is sounding and looking a lot like foreplay," Kyle said to Chaz.

"I was thinking the same thing," Chaz replied.

"What's foreplay?" Mark asked, pulling our attention to him.

"Um," Kyle said, his eyes bugging out a bit.

"It's kind of like an appetizer for grownups," Chaz said after realizing that Kyle was at a loss for words. "We'll have this conversation in a few more years."

"So, it's about sex then. Gross!" Mark's queasy expression made me smile. The look of horror turned to pure joy when he saw the Dorchesters approach. "Daniel!"

Daniel Dorchester smiled just as broadly when he spotted

Mark. The boys greeted each other with a big hug then walked ahead of us with their arms looped together as we headed to the hot chocolate booth.

"I see its more than just Kyle and Chaz's affection that's contributing to Mark's remarkable turnaround," I said cheerfully. "I'm so glad he made a fast friend with Daniel."

"We're pretty sure it's more than friendship for Daniel," John said with a rueful smile. "I don't remember hugging my friends like that." I expected Deanna to comment, but she remained silent. She had been open and loving to Mark the minute she met him, so I knew that her silence had zero to do with him being transgender. John looped his arm around Deanna's neck and kissed her temple affectionately before he said, "Someone isn't ready for her firstborn to fall in love."

Deanna sniffed and briefly covered her face with her gloves. "I'm supposed to be the love of his life for another few years."

"No one will ever replace you in his heart," John said softly to his wife.

"I know," she sniffed once more before smiling up at Chaz and Kyle. "At least he'll have great in-laws."

"Whoa!" Chaz said, covering his heart like she'd stabbed him in the chest. "We're not ready for that either. Hell, we just got our first kid and you're marrying him off already."

"It's not going to be easy for them," Kyle said soberly as we watched the two boys interact. "I just want to protect them from the bullshit they'll face outside our tightknit group."

"Nothing worth having ever comes easy," I remarked. "Besides, they have a soft, safe place to land with all of us."

The line for the hot chocolate was long, but the two boys didn't seem to mind. They talked nonstop, often over top of one another, as they waited. Two older boys, I assumed to be high school age, homed in on Mark and Daniel with disgust in their eyes. They started to step forward but a tall, dangerous looking man stepped in front of them before they got too close to the kids.

"Or, Jon can make them disappear," Josh offered.

Jon stepped forward and the troublemakers staggered back a few steps. I couldn't hear what Jon said, but I guessed it was very descriptive judging by the ghost-white expressions on the older boys' faces. Emory shook his head slowly, but his smile said he heartily approved of his fiancé's message.

Mark and Daniel worked their way to the front of the line without knowing that trouble had been lurking around them. We couldn't always be with them, so their parents would need to sit them down and have a conversation about being aware of their surroundings. That made me irrationally angry. What kind of world did we live in? Why couldn't those kids just be kids and not have to worry about bullies and beatings? I remembered how scarred Josh was when I first met him because of cruel idiots and that made me even madder. It didn't help when I spotted my nemesis nearby with Dare on his arm.

"What the fuck is that?" I snarled, nodding my head in Doctor Douche's direction.

"The reason why I had to cut Trent's hair," Josh replied. Sure enough, Wren wasn't too far behind them, watching the couple walk slowly through the crowd. "I'm pretty sure Wren is going to need bail money."

"Who said I would arrest him?" I asked. "I wonder if it's too late to accept Jon's generous offer to help relocate the doctor."

"Gabe, stop," Josh said in frustration. "And watch what you say around our babies. They'll go to preschool talking like Tony Soprano's grandchildren." Okay, he had a point.

"You have to admit that his hair looks better after I got ahold of it."

"I'll do no such thing," I replied.

It was obvious that the close call with the bullies dampened our Christmas spirit by the time we reached Mark, Daniel, Jon, and Emory. I didn't think anyone was in the mood to tour through Santa's remodeled village, so I made a different suggestion after looking at my watch. "Why don't we all go back to our place and watch *Rudolph*, eat some cookies, and drink milk or hot chocolate."

The kids were all for it, but there were mixed reactions from the adults. Not everyone was a kid at heart when it came to Christmas movies. "Josh can lace the adults' hot chocolate with brandy or make that boozy buttered rum beverage I found on Pinterest," I offered without consulting my husband first.

"*Pinterest?*" Jon asked. I heard the censure in his voice, but he'd eat—or drink—his words after he tried one of those drinks.

"Yeah, you heard me, Silver." I leaned forward and said, "You can find everything there from decorating, to cooking, to what gets blood out of—"

"Gabe."

"I was going to say clothes, Sunshine. You know how hard I am on my baseball pants." I tipped my head in Jon's direction. "Doubtful he needs training on that particular skillset though."

"I've learned that fire works wonderfully," Jon said with a devilish grin.

Emory elbowed him playfully in the ribs. "He also thinks it's a suitable way to kill spiders," Emory teased. "I had to explain to him that our insurance company wouldn't agree."

"That spider was the size of my fist *and* it jumped." Jon shivered hard as he recalled the incident.

Jon was afraid of spiders. That was good to know for future torment and gag gifts.

"What's the name of that website again?" Jon asked after he took his first sip of Josh's creamy, buttered rum drink. "This is ridiculously good."

"And messy," Emory said, wiping off a glob of cream that stuck to the corner of Jon's mouth. Instead of wiping it on a napkin, Emory sucked it off his finger like he would if he got chocolate icing on it. He wasn't intentionally trying to be sexy, but I could see it had the same effect on Jon.

"Ready to go home? It's past your bedtime," Jon remarked.

"Since when?" Emory asked. "*Rudolph* just started."

"We can watch it at home." Jon pressed his lips against Emory's ear and said something else. Em's blush told me that it was a rather dirty suggestion.

"I *am* feeling tired," Emory said, but looked longingly at his hot, boozy drink.

"I can pour it in a to-go cup for you," Josh offered.

"Perfect!" Jon exclaimed.

The warm booze helped me to relax and enjoy the show with our extended family. Destiny and Dylan fell asleep long before Rudolph reached the island of misfit toys. Our parents took the kids up to bed and retired early themselves. Josh climbed onto my vacated lap and snuggled against my chest. Meredith had assumed the same position in the recliner with Harley while Kyle and Chaz shared the love seat. Sally Ann cuddled into Adrian's side as he held a sleeping Avery against his chest. Mark and Daniel sat on the floor in front of John and Deanna, holding hands and whispering to each other, while the rest of the Dorchester kids and Adrianna lay on their stomachs watching Rudolph's adventures unfold.

It was Norman Rockwell 2.0 with traditions that involved the modern family. It was everything I dreamed it would be and more. We might just need to buy more furniture to accommodate our expanding families.

"Chet's nuts roasting on an open fire," Savage crooned from his perch.

"Who's Chet?" Harley asked.

"Don't know," Mere replied sleepily, "but I feel bad for him."

Josh turned his head and looked at me over his shoulder. "Did you teach him that?"

"No," I scoffed, but damn if that bird didn't give me a good idea.

I didn't get a chance to put my plan into motion until after our guests left and Josh went up to bed. I told him I was double-checking to make sure all the doors were locked, but I wanted to have a little one-on-one time with my boy, Savage. Like always, my feathered friend caught on fast. The only unpredictable part was when he'd say it on his own.

"Gabe!" Josh called from the stairs. "I know that you're up to no good. If you're going to be bad, do it naked with me."

"Coming, dear."

"Do you want pancakes or French toast?" Josh asked me the next morning. I looked around the kitchen and saw that we were all alone because the grandparents took the grandbabies on an excursion. I had much better things on my mind than food. "Eat up, Gabriel. You're going to need your energy because I have some last-minute shopping at the mall to do before your tattoo appointment."

I groaned as my appetite disappeared over the most dreadful words in the English language. "I don't want to go shopping at the mall." Yeah, I whined like a three-year-old kid. "Why can't we drive separately and meet at Dream Ink?"

"Our children are having their pictures taken with Santa in just a little bit. You know damn well that you don't want to miss it. While I'm there, I might as well pick up the few things left on my list." Josh pointed his spatula at me and added, "I let you sleep in late to rest up for the big day. Now behave."

"I don't want to behave."

"I'll reward you handsomely later."

"Yeah? What are you going to do to me?" *Hey, people have used sex to get their way since the beginning of time. Why the fuck should I be any different?*

"Trent's nuts roasting on an open fire," Savage sang from his solarium. *Fuck!*

"I'm going to kill you, Gabe. Then I'm going to get advice from Pinterest on how to cover up my crime."

"Now, Sunshine," I said pleadingly.

"Up those stairs and get dressed, Gabriel!" *Uh oh.* "It appears that we have extra time to get more shopping in since I won't be riding your cock reverse cowboy style before we go." Josh pointed toward the staircase, indicating that I was supposed to march up those steps and do what he said, but he used two of my favorite words in the English dictionary: reverse cowboy.

I pulled my shirt over my head and tossed it to the floor in answer to his demands.

"We're not having sex in the kitchen, Gabriel." Oh, I loved that bossy fucking tone of voice.

My response was to remove my sweats and underwear. "How much do you want to bet?" I asked, stroking my erection. "Just think of how much better I'll behave if you bring that hot ass over here and fuck me into behaving."

"I'm not rewarding your bad behavior with sex."

"Since when?"

"Right now," Josh said adamantly, but his smoldering eyes said something different.

I reached between my legs with my free hand and cupped my balls while working my swollen knob with the other. "Come over here."

"I'm not in the mood." His stubbornness was adorable, but his erection tenting his pj pants called him a liar. "Oh, fuck it!" Josh threw his spatula on the counter then jumped me.

I might've been joking before about him fucking me into behaving, but he wrung me out so much that I didn't have the energy to put up a fight at the mall. We made it in time to see our kids scream the building down when the grandmas tried to set them on Santa's lap. Maybe it was sick of me, but I suspected that would be my favorite moment of the season.

FOURTEEN

Josh

IT SEEMED THAT THINGS WERE FINALLY GOING TO SETTLE DOWN A bit the week before Christmas, which was the opposite of what you'd expect. Most people start getting frantic when the days until Christmas reached the single digits, but not me. Hey, I had every right to be hysterical while juggling a busy schedule at the salon, the 'rents staying at our house, and Gabe's nightly countdown to the perfect Christmas activities. It sounded like a huge cluster-fuck, but it was the most magical time of my life.

With that said, I decided to put my size nine Converse down that night and insist we have quiet evenings at home leading up to my annual Ugly Christmas Sweater party. Besides, what the hell else was there left to do? I knew that Gabe would balk, but I planned to distract him with a grown-up version of a Christmas advent calendar. I got the idea from the countdown advent calendar I received from my secret Santa at the salon. It had Christmas giftboxes wrapped in festive, shiny green paper that stacked to form the shape of a tree. Each box was numbered from twenty-five down to one and was just big enough to hold a few pieces of candy or a little trinket.

My favorite gift so far was a tiny picture frame attached to a keychain. The picture frame was nearly an exact replica of the gilded glamorous ones I had at my station. The picture inside wasn't the typical family photo though. It was two dads having to sit on the mall Santa's lap before their babies would trust the stranger with bright red clothes and that fake-as-fuck, white beard. Gabe and I were laughing, the babies were screaming, and Santa looked ready to hit the bottle. I loved it so much that I would've used it for the photo on our Christmas card if I'd had it in time.

Up until I opened that gift, I thought Meredith drew my name from the Santa hat, but that gift had Gabriel Roman-Wyatt stamped all over it. It didn't surprise me that he joined in on the salon festivities because he was a Christmas freak and half-owner of Curl Up and Dye. I started to suspect that him having my name was more than simple luck of the draw. It was too late to swap names to get his, so I decided to spring a surprise on him at home that would accomplish two things: have fun and wear us both out. An exhausted Gabe was one who didn't drag me around to every outdoor manger in a thirty-mile radius. Oh, holy night, I needed a break.

Surprising Gabe kept my spirits up during the long day. In fact, I didn't even mind when Trent showed up midday to take

Dare to lunch. Wren minded a lot though. Those two guys were making me nuts, but there was nothing I could do about it except knock their heads together. The idea grew in merit each day that the tension grew between the two men. I didn't want to accuse Dare of using Trent to make Wren jealous, but he sure as hell didn't look at Trent the way he looked at Wren. *Stay out of it. Stay out of it. Stay out of it.*

Repeating that in my head over and over helped, until Dare approached me that night with a nervous expression on his face. No one on my staff feared me for crying out loud. I was the best damn boss on the planet, yet Dare looked like he was seconds away from pissing down his leg. What could be so…

"It's not a good idea," I said when I realized what he wanted to ask. The crestfallen look on Dare's face made me feel terrible, and I thought perhaps he liked Dr. Doofus more than I had originally thought. "Okay, let me talk to Gabe."

"You're the best, Josh," Dare said, hugging me. "I'm going to start planning our ugly sweaters because there's no way Gabe can tell you no."

"No fucking way," Gabe said, shaking his head.

I looked up from stirring the pot of stew that Martina had started earlier in the day. Gabe sat in a kitchen chair with a baby on both knees. "I haven't even asked a question yet."

"I can tell by your expression that you're going to ask something I won't like, and I can bet what it is since we're only a few days away from the annual Christmas party for our friends and salon family." *Do you see why I love him so much? Not salon employees. Not salon staff. Family!* "The answer is no."

There comes a time in every man's life where he needs to

learn to choose his battles or be miserable. Now, I could've pointed out that Gabe's ex-lover, one he lived with for a few years, sat at our table and ate our food week after week, and I never once complained or got jealous. I would've been justified in doing so, and maybe I would've taken up the fight if Dare had convinced me that Trent was the one for him, but I saw the smug smirk Dare gave Wren after talking to me. Therefore, I chose not to call Gabe out on his knuckle-dragging bullshit.

"I was going to ask if you wanted to top or bottom tonight, Captain Know-It-All." *I said I pick my battles; I didn't say anything about giving Gabe a bigger ego than he already had.*

Gabe threw his head back and laughed. "God, you're such a bad liar."

"That's a bad thing?"

Gabe tipped his head and thought for a second. "Not at all, but I do wonder how the hell you keep beating everyone at poker."

"I'm a Gemini, Gabe. Multi-faceted. Chameleon. Awesome." I put the lid back on the pot and walked over to the loves of my life. After I kissed each baby on the forehead and Gabe firmly on the lips, I said, "I need to go make a quick phone call before dinner." I thought it was best not to have the conversation at the salon the next morning, and I wanted to give all my energy to Gabe and the babies after dinner.

"Tell Dare that he's playing with fire," Gabe called out to me.

I went to the library slash office to call Dare and was glad when he answered right away. "So, look—"

"Hell has frozen over," Dare said, interrupting me. "Gabe actually told you no."

"He really hates Trent, and to be honest, I'm not all that comfortable around him either. Trent has apologized for the way he treated me, and I even think he means it."

"But he still makes you uncomfortable," Dare added. "Kind of like a reminder of a bad time in your life." His voice had softened to nearly a whisper at the end. "Oh man."

"What?" I asked.

"I think that's what I am for Wren. I remind him of something or someone unpleasant."

"I doubt it, Dare. You're so delightful to be around," I told him.

"No, it makes perfectly good sense. There have been a few occasions that he briefly dropped his guard, and I saw that he wanted me. Something holds him back."

"It probably doesn't have anything to do with you." I thought back to the way I battled my feelings for Gabe. Yes, our initial meeting was a disaster, but Gabe had attempted to apologize many times afterward. I wouldn't let him because it was easier to hold him at bay when I was pissed. "I think he's fighting himself, not you. Would you like some advice from someone who's probably been in a similar headspace as Wren?"

"That would be great."

"Don't play games with him, Dare. If you really want a shot with Wren, you'll have to be patient and show him that you're worth the risk. Sometimes you have to wear them down with your patience." I smiled as I recalled Gabe doing just that. "When he pushes you away, give him space to breathe, but don't ever give up. Prove to him that you're someone he can rely on and a person who will care for *all* of him, even the parts he doesn't like. I'm not asking you to let him push you around by any means, because he needs to respect you and your feelings."

Dare blew out a shaky breath. "He has the power to destroy me, Josh."

He sounded so conflicted, and I wished I could give him a hug, but had to settle for verbal reassurance. "He probably thinks the same about you, cutie. You need to figure out what you want and then go after it. If your heart chooses Wren, then you drop this pretense with Trent and focus your time and energy on the man you want. While it might be cute when Wren goes all cave-man over the doctor, it's not good for him, and it's no way to begin a relationship."

"Relationship," Dare repeated reverently. There was no doubt in my mind who Dare really wanted. Did he possess the mental toughness and tenacity it took to win Wren's trust and heart? Only time would tell. "I want what you and Gabe have."

I chuckled. "Then you'll take my advice to heart, my friend. Gabe did all the things that I described, and I knew that my heart was safe with him. He showed me a life I never dreamed possible, and, Dare, there's nothing I wouldn't do for him."

Dare sighed sappily. "Thank you, Josh. I'm sorry that I asked if Trent could come to the party with me. It was really selfish, and I didn't mean to disrespect Gabe."

"I know that, Dare. I'm glad we could have this conversation though."

"Me too. See you in the morning."

"Goodnight."

I just stood in the peaceful library for a few minutes after I hung up, hoping that I did the right thing by giving Dare advice. I should've stayed out of it, but I hated to see a beautiful opportunity wasted by miscommunication.

"Dinner is ready," Gabe said softly.

I whirled around and found him leaning in the doorway. "How long have you been standing there?" His posture was casual, but the heat in his eyes was anything but, so I suspected he overheard most of what I said to Dare, if not all. Gabe straightened then crossed the room to cup my face.

"You gave the kid good advice, Sunshine." Oh, how I loved the deep timbre of his voice and the look of adoration in his dark brown eyes. "We've sure had our ups and downs, but I'd do it all over again."

He could still render me speechless, but that was okay, because

I showed him how much his words meant to me with a kiss. Lord, that man knew how to make me melt. I eagerly waited for the moment that we could go upstairs to the privacy of our room, so he could open his naughty Santa advent calendar.

Gabe pulled back from our kiss and ran his thumb over my wet lips. "Let's eat dinner because I have a surprise for us."

I groaned. "Babe, can't we stay home tonight. We can watch *Die Hard* after Destiny and Dylan go to bed. We'll watch it naked," I tossed out as an added incentive.

"We can do all of the above," Gabe assured me as he tugged my reluctant ass toward the kitchen. "My excursion won't take long."

Thirty minutes later, Gabe packed us all in the Grandparent's Express minivan. Al sat up front with Gabe because he was too tall to ride in the back. I wedged myself between the two car seats, while my parents and Martina climbed into the third row.

"Everyone buckled up? This sleigh is pulling out," Gabe said cheerfully.

I rolled my eyes then glared at him in the rearview mirror. "Did you rent this bright red minivan on purpose?" I asked my parents.

"Pure coincidence," my mom replied. "Sure is snazzy though. Plenty of room. Your father and I are going to buy one and drive it here when we move. Well, I'll drive the van while he drives the moving truck."

"Still not giving up on that idea?" I jokingly asked my mom.

"You couldn't be so lucky," she teased as she ruffled my hair.

"Are we there yet?" I whined to Gabe before we made it to the end of our street.

"No cookies and hot chocolate for you tonight, Bad Daddy," Gabe said.

"Yet, Papa? Yet?" Destiny repeated, reminding me of Savage.

"Yet? Bad Daddy!" Dylan said, waving his little fists in the air.

"Gabe!" The last thing I wanted was my kids calling me Bad Daddy in public.

"I was just teasing, Dylan. Good Daddy, not Bad Daddy."

"Bad Daddy!" both twins said.

Gabe bit his lip to keep from laughing, but I wasn't amused. Hell, I would've preferred Little Daddy over Bad Daddy. I was going to smash that advent calendar to bits, but only after Gabe saw what he was missing out on.

"Good Daddy," the grandparents all said as if they sensed the storm brewing inside me.

"Bad Daddy!" Dylan and Destiny countered.

No matter how many times someone called me Good Daddy, the kids kept insisting I was Bad Daddy. They giggled and squealed like happy babies do, especially when I pretended to cry. I realized they were treating it as a game. Instead of launching their sippy cups off their high chairs just so Gabe or I would pick them up, they teased me to get a dramatic reaction. So, I used reverse psychology and referred to myself as bad so that they would call me good. It worked beautifully and I figuratively patted myself on the back.

"Where are we going exactly?" I asked.

"Wen told me about this subdivision in a neighboring community that goes all out for the holidays. Every house is decorated with a theme, and he said that some of the displays flicker in time to music."

"Oh man," I said, certain that Gabe would be taking notes for a future display.

"We'll blow them away next year, Gabe," my father said, rubbing his hands together.

"You know it, Dad."

We weren't the only ones driving out to see the neighborhood light displays that night. Cars were backed up down the street for a good mile and a half and the spectators creeped along at a snail's pace. Our babies were sound asleep before we even turned on the street, but Gabe lit up as bright as the displays. His childlike enthusiasm made me ridiculously happy, and I forgot all about punishing him.

My dad and Gabe chatted nonstop on the trip home about all the things they wanted to do next year and how they thought they could achieve it. All that excitement came to a screeching halt when we turned down our street and noticed that our house wasn't lit up like it had been when we left.

"We've been hit by the Christmas Bandits!" Gabe said. Our moms took the babies inside while the rest of us checked out the damage.

Sure enough, someone had come along and cut the electrical cords where they plugged into the outlets, stole our big, beautiful wreath off the front door, and busted the glass snowmen on the porch.

"Can you believe the balls on these guys?" Gabe snarled. "They vandalized the police captain's house? Merry Fucking Christmas to you too, assholes. Laugh it up while you can because I'm going to find you," he yelled into the night.

Uh oh. Gabe was about to go John McClane on somebody!

FIFTEEN

Gabe

"THE CHRISTMAS BANDITS HIT TEN MORE HOUSES LAST NIGHT besides yours, Cap," Wen said. "This is getting out of control."

"It has to be young punks with nothing better to do with their time," Adrian commented.

"Do you think it's the same group of burglars and vandals?" Wen asked. "The crimes are different but their ability to move around town quietly without getting caught is the same."

"I guess it's possible," Adrian said, but he didn't sound

convinced. "Typically, people's crimes escalate, not de-escalate."

"Boredom? Easy targets?" Wen asked.

"Anything is possible," Adrian replied.

I pinched the bridge of my nose as I tried to figure out what I should do next. I'd already held a town hall meeting for fuck's sake and increased patrol officer presence. These little fuckers were always a step ahead of me.

My cell phone lit up with an incoming call from Josh, and I welcomed the interruption to my downward spiraling thoughts. "Miss me already, Sunshine?" I said into the phone.

"I've been hit!" Josh said frantically.

"What?" My heart nearly exploded in my chest as my mind raced through all the horrible possibilities. "Oh my God! Are you okay? Where are you? I'll be right there!"

"What do you mean? I'm at the salon. Where'd you think I was?" The anger in his voice dwindled to irritation.

"You said you were hit, so I thought you were involved in a car accident." I was going to turn him over my knee and spank his ass for scaring the fuck out of me like that.

"Baby, I'm sorry," Josh said softly. "I didn't mean to scare you. I'm just pissed off."

His tenderness mollified my thundering heart a little bit, but I wasn't ready to forgive him yet. "What happened?"

"The Christmas Bandits hit the salon last night," he said. "Christmas lights cut and the pretty wreaths my mom made twenty years ago were stolen."

"All of them?" I asked.

"Yes!"

Bertie had made enough wreaths to decorate the entire wraparound porch on the salon. Each wreath had a pair of white ice skates in the center and were adorned with white lights and red bows. Josh inspected each pair of skates to make sure they were a pristine white before Bill and I strategically hung them around the porch. "Every third post," Josh had reminded me. "Hang them too close and they just look tacky. The Roman-Wyatts don't do tacky decorations." I knew they meant a lot to him because he even kept a bottle of white shoe polish handy to touch up the skates when needed.

"What kind of monster does this, Gabe? Those wreaths have hung on that porch longer than I've been alive!"

"I'll get your wreaths back, Sunshine. I promise."

"Damn straight you will, Captain Kick Ass. In the meantime, I'm going to call a few of the local business owners to see if they'll join me in offering a reward for the capture of the Christmas Bandits."

"Great idea," I told him. "Let me know what they say, and I'll announce it in the local newspaper."

"I'll offer up a thousand-dollar reward by myself if I need to; I want my wreaths back."

"You arrange for the funds, and I'll take care of the rest. We'll get them back."

"We make a great team." I heard the smile in Josh's voice.

I suspected he was remembering the activities from the previous evening. I needed an outlet for my frustration and Josh provided the perfect distraction with his naughty secret Santa countdown thingy. I think I surprised us both when I chose to wear the silky red mask and submit myself to Josh and the soft, red feather.

"In all things, Sunshine." I heard Adrian clear his throat and Wen chuckle, which meant that either my voice or expression hinted to where my mind had gone. "Adrian and Wen are in my office and they think we're having phone sex instead of discussing a heinous crime committed against you. I'm going to send Wen over there to take a statement and photograph the crime scene so that you can file an official report. I can't look like I'm playing favorites."

Wen grinned and shook his head. "On it, Cap."

138

"Adrian gets to compile the data from all the reported crimes into a program, so we can determine peak times or even days of the week. The slightest similarity could bust the case wide open."

Adrian sighed heavily, but followed Wen out the door without complaint.

"Are you alone now?" Josh whispered into the phone.

My brain and dick perked up. "Yes. What did you have in mind?"

"Just you wait and see what I have in store for us tonight."

"Do you remember how everyone cautioned us not to go overboard with holidays and birthdays for our kids because they'd come to expect it and we'd put pressure on ourselves to keep outdoing the previous years?" I asked Josh.

"Yes." I knew Josh had zero intention of listening to that particular piece of advice. We would do things our way and to hell with what people thought.

"That logic doesn't apply here, Sunshine. I'm going to need you to step this up each year from now on."

"I accept that challenge, Gabe." I heard Dare calling for Josh in the background. "My client is here, so I have to go. I'll call you in a bit after I've had a chance to drum up support for the reward money. I love you."

"Love you, too."

After I disconnected the call with Josh, I went in search of Adrian. I was half-joking when I mentioned the program because I wanted to razz him, but it gave me another idea.

"It's time to go John McClane on these fuckers!" I told Adrian.

"What brings you by the newspaper, Captain?" Myrna Evans asked me a few hours later.

The first time I'd met her, Billy Sampson had dropped off an anonymous letter informing the Blissville Daily News that the police department wasn't treating his threats against Josh seriously. That seemed like decades ago, but in reality, not even two years had passed since then.

"I'd like your help capturing the Christmas Bandits," I told the editor.

"Oh, how exciting." Myrna sat straighter in her chair. "What can I do?"

"Some of the local businesses are pooling resources and offering a reward for the tip that leads to arresting the bandits."

"That's a good idea," Myrna said. "Money is a big motivator."

"Five thousand dollars is one hell of an incentive."

"Wow! Are you serious?"

I nodded my head. "Ten businesses are chipping in five hundred bucks each."

"That's amazing, Captain. Do you just want to place a large ad in the paper for the next few days?"

"Yes, but I'd like to go a step further if you're willing to listen to my idea," I said.

"Of course. What did you have in mind?"

"Detective Goode compiled a lot of data from the reports and it pinpoints some consistencies between days and times these crimes occur."

"Crimes?" Myrna asked. "I get that people are annoyed, but is this really a crime? We're talking about someone cutting Christmas lights and poking holes in inflatable snowmen that no one likes anyway, right? That's just a silly misdemeanor, isn't it?"

"Looking at the cases individually, they might not look like much, but we're talking grand theft and criminal mischief when you add up all of the stolen and damaged items."

"Grand theft?" she asked in shock. "That much has been stolen or damaged?"

"Yes, ma'am," I told her. "We're talking fourth and fifth degree felonies. And if I can link them to the other thefts and burglaries…"

"Holy hell. This is much bigger than I thought." Myrna leaned forward. "How can I help you catch these assholes?"

"First, we need to change the notion that it's just a few cut Christmas lights and deflated snowmen that no one likes anyway." At least the editor had the good grace to look embarrassed by her earlier remark. "We need to make this a human-interest story, give it a face that people know and recognize. Some of these people lost items that had been in their families for decades, Myrna."

Josh wasn't the only one who had meaningful items taken. Another resident had an antique sled stolen right off her front porch. Her grandfather handcrafted it for her father when he was a small boy nearly seventy years ago. She put it out each year with fake Christmas presents on it to decorate her porch.

"I'm sorry that I took such a cavalier attitude toward the crimes. I wasn't aware that it had gotten so serious. I mean, I knew you hosted a town hall meeting about it, but apparently I didn't get it even after that."

"Now you know, and now you can help."

I could've assigned anyone on the police department or even asked for civilian volunteers to hang the reward posters all over town, but I did it myself. Partly because I wanted the town to know how seriously we were taking the crimes, and partly as penance for not doing more sooner.

"You're going to need a designated tip line," Milo told me when I stopped by Books and Brew. He gestured toward the group of teenagers who had gathered around the sign I hung in the window before I placed my order. They talked excitedly amongst themselves and looked to be forming a plan.

Maegan joined us at the counter with my order. "Oh look, it's Nancy Drew and The Hardy Boys!" She shook her head and said, "This could be the best five hundred dollars we ever spent."

"The local paper is printing the name of the local businesses who are offering reward money. I think you guys should be recognized."

"It's our pleasure," Milo replied then nodded at the two carryout trays in front of me. "These should help sweeten Josh's day."

"I hope so."

"Do you want some help carrying those out?" Maegan asked.

"Nah," I said dismissively. "I'm used to juggling two babies, two diaper bags, and whatever we need for our excursions. What's eight cups of coffee compared to all that?"

Maegan laughed and said, "At least let me open the door for you."

"Yeah, I'm used to people showing me to the door too."

"I hope you have a great night, Gabe," Maegan said, patting me on the shoulder as I passed through the door.

Oh, I planned on it. "Same to you, Maegan."

I managed to get the eight cups of coffee to the salon without making a liar of myself. It wasn't that the salon didn't have a coffee maker, but nothing was better than a special treat in the afternoon, especially after the crappy way Josh's day started. I couldn't treat Josh and neglect the rest of our salon family.

I handed soy vanilla lattes to Dee and Josi, white chocolate lattes to Marci and Dare, straight-up black coffee to Wren and Heather, a salted caramel to my man, and chamomile tea to Mere.

The ladies hugged me, Dare patted my shoulder, Wren grunted appreciatively, and Josh gave me a quick peck on the lips. I wanted to drag him off to the mixing room for a proper kiss, but I didn't want to mess up his mojo.

"See you at home," I tossed over my shoulder on my way out

the door.

I had planned to stop by the station long enough to read my messages and find out if we had any tips come in yet, but one look at the harried expressions on the officers in the station nixed the idea of leaving early.

"Any calls come in?" I asked hesitantly.

"Any calls?" Officer O'Malley asked. "Try two hundred."

"Two hundred? Those posters haven't been up for more than an hour," I said in shock. "Are they legitimate calls?"

"Aliens are the culprits, Captain," Officer Wen said. "They're taking the items back to their planet to study us in preparation for conquering Earth."

"Traveling gypsies," Murkowsky countered then flipped through her notebook. "Atheists, Scientologists…"

"Jehovah's Witnesses," Officer Jones added.

"No, it's the Baptists," Officer Kasey countered her partner.

"There have been a few legitimate calls, Cap," Adrian said. "I'm heading out to check on a few things."

"Take Wen with you," I told him.

The phone never stopped ringing the entire time my officers filled me in on the tips they'd received so far. Instead of going home, I took off my coat and sat at my old desk with a pad of paper and a pen. An effective leader held fast to a basic rule: never ask people to do things you're unwilling to do yourself.

I wrote down the names of each caller I spoke with and included their contact number in case their lead panned out. I didn't really think that Jerry Springer or Oprah were behind the thefts and vandalism, but wrote the information down the same. I figured the calls would settle down over the next few days, but until then, it looked like I would need to authorize overtime.

I sent Josh a text and told him that I'd be home late, expecting to work an extra hour or two. Instead, I pulled into the driveway after eleven o'clock. There were only a few lights left on so that I could find my way through the first floor and up the stairs without killing myself. Josh was sound asleep in our bed with Buddy acting as guard by his feet.

"I'll take it from here, boy," I told him.

Buddy jumped down and retreated to his dog bed near the fireplace while I quickly undressed and carelessly tossed my clothes on the floor. I might catch hell from Josh the next morning, but I was exhausted from the long day, pissy that I didn't get home in time to put my kids to bed, and frustrated that I missed my naughty countdown surprise.

All those cantankerous emotions faded the minute I slid beneath the sheets and snuggled up to my warm, naked husband. Josh turned in the circle of my arms and nuzzled his nose in the hollow of my collarbone.

"Did you catch him?" Josh asked groggily.

"Nope," I said into the darkness. "Tomorrow is a new day."

"Missed you tonight."

"I missed you guys too. Did anything important happen?"

"Dylan said his first curse word."

"Shit!"

"Well, technically it was 'fuh-nug,' but I'm pretty sure we know what he was trying to say." He laughed against my chest, and I held him tighter. "We're not supposed to laugh, Gabe."

"I'm not the one laughing," I pointed out.

"You would be if you heard that precious little voice curse." Josh snickered some more. "My favorite part is that he used it in the right context." His light laughter turned into full-bellied laughs as he recalled the incident.

"Are you going to share?" I asked irritably. I hated that I missed my son's first curse word.

"He dropped his cookie on the floor and Buddy ate it. I'm not sure if he said it because he was mad or he cursed the dog, but either way it was fucking hilarious. I had to sternly say, 'Dylan

James we don't talk like that in this house, just the birds do.' Then I had to leave the room so that he wouldn't see or hear me laugh. Our dads came with me and we laughed until we cried."

"Damn, I wish I was here."

"I'm pretty sure you'll have plenty of opportunities to correct salty language."

"Good."

"You know what else is good?" Josh asked.

"I get two surprises tomorrow?" I asked hopefully.

"Why wait? Do you trust me?"

"Of course."

I felt him rooting around beneath our pillows then heard a soft buzzing sound when he pulled his hand free. Funny how alert a man could become when his husband pressed a small vibrating object against his taint.

"Oh, holy night, Sunshine."

SIXTEEN

Josh

I WOKE UP WITH A HAPPY SMILE ON MY FACE AND IT REMAINED there even after I stepped on Gabe's belt buckle and tripped over one of his shoes. I couldn't be angry with him because I knew he was exhausted when he got home and just wanted to get in bed with me. It helped that he sent me back into dreamland with curled toes and a sappy grin on my face like the one I saw in the mirror when I brushed my teeth.

I didn't lose my good humor until I got downstairs and saw

that I had two droopy babies on my hands. Their misery was obvious in their eyes and it broke my heart. I pressed the back of my hands to Dylan's forehead and he had a fever. Destiny was clammy and damp like her fever had just broken.

"My poor angels," I said, snatching them from their grandmothers and holding them against my chest. "Colds?" I asked the in-house experts.

"That's what we suspect," Martina said. "They're not teething."

"I gave them a dose of the infant Tylenol I found in the cabinet," my mom said. "They both sound a little congested, so you might want to call the pediatrician's office to see what they recommend for them to take."

"This isn't our first rodeo with colds, is it, babies?" I looked at the moms and said, "I have just the thing. If it doesn't work then we'll call the doctor for a medicine recommendation, but I'd like to try a natural method first." The grandmothers followed me up to the nursery where I kept the eucalyptus tummy rub I made for them the last time they were congested.

"Is this like a homeopathic version of Vicks?" Martina asked when she smelled the contents of the jar.

"Yep. They don't recommend Vicks for children under the age of two, and I'm not crazy about giving my babies over-the-counter meds because they contain chemicals that make their hearts race."

"You never could take decongestants very well," my mom said. "Do you use this on yourself?"

"I don't get sick, but I smeared it on Gabe the last time he had sinus congestion. He wanted to fight me on it, but he thanked me later after he could breathe again." *Boy, did he ever.* "Mom, can you get the humidifier from the closet and add a few drops of the eucalyptus oil to the water? That'll help too."

"Sure," both moms said then laughed.

Martina pulled the humidifier down while my mom retrieved the essential oil.

"We can also put a tiny dab of Vaseline in their noses to ease the dryness in their nasal passages," I told them.

I stripped Destiny down to her diaper and smeared the concoction of coconut and eucalyptus oils on her tiny little chest. When I was done, Martina took her from me to dress her so I could see to Dylan.

"Papa," Destiny said when Gabe entered the room, but she didn't sound her normal cheery self.

"What's going on?" Gabe asked, rubbing the sleep from his eyes. He sniffed the air. "Do my precious angels have a cold?"

"Looks like it," I answered. "We're going to try a natural method first, and if that doesn't work, then I'll call the pediatrician's office to see what they recommend."

"It worked great last time," Gabe commented as he joined me. He dipped two fingers into the glass jar and spread it on Dylan's chest. "Didn't it, big guy?"

"Papa," Dylan whined pitifully.

"His fever hasn't broken yet, so we need to wrap him up and get him warm."

"I know the best place in the house for babies who don't feel good," Gabe suggested.

"With their grandmas," Martina said. "Both of you have work to do, so Bertie and I will take over. I can already hear the difference in their breathing."

Gabe and I looked at each other uncertainly. Neither of us wanted to go to work with the kids sick at home, but we both had busy days ahead of us. "Yeah, okay," I said reluctantly, "but we want you to check in every half hour or so."

"Or hourly," Gabe said after the moms pinned us with incredulous looks.

"We nursed you back to good health plenty of times," my mom said. "Now go get ready for work."

Neither of us were happy about it, but we knew they were

right. We weren't the only working parents who would rather stay home with their sick kids than trudge into work. It seemed like the new normal was feeling guilty all the time. At work, you thought about all the things waiting for you at home, but when you got home, you worried about the things you didn't finish at work. It was a constant juggling act that Gabe and I managed well, but sick babies at home wasn't the same as forgetting to put the clothes in the dryer. I would worry about them all damn day, and I knew Gabe would also.

We peeked in on them in their nursery before we left. They were sound asleep in their grandmothers' arms and didn't even stir when we kissed them goodbye.

"Dylan's fever broke," my mom said. "They're going to be just fine."

Gabe pulled me to him for a lingering kiss before I could climb in my SUV. "I'll get home at a decent time tonight," he promised me. "I'm sure things will be calmer at the police station today."

"Let's hope so."

It wasn't often that someone arrived at the salon before me, but Wren beat me in that morning.

"Everything okay?" he asked when I walked through the back door.

"The twins have colds," I replied as I tipped my head and studied him. There was something different about Wren, but what? He wore his typical long-sleeved gray t-shirt, black jeans, and black biker boots. He hadn't shaved his beard or cut his long hair. *Aha!* I mentally snapped my fingers. His hair hung to his shoulders when it was usually tied back when he worked.

Wren snorted and said, "Bet you'll avoid the doctor's office like the plague since Dr. Douche is working there."

"Oh man, I hadn't thought about that. Let's hope my homeopathic efforts work."

Wren grinned wryly. "I'll cross my fingers for you."

"Good morning," Dare said when he entered the salon. He was all toothy grins and happiness while Wren grew rigid and red-faced. *Hmmmm, what had happened between these two?*

Wren turned his head to look at Dare and I got a glimpse of the reason why Wren had chosen to wear his hair down. I sent up a prayer that Dare was the one who left that little love bite low on Wren's neck. I got my answer when Dare crossed over to him and looked at his handiwork.

"I can cover that with concealer if you prefer to wear your hair up," Dare offered.

"Nah."

I could tell that the guys could use a few minutes alone before the crazy set in, so I excused myself to make a cup of coffee and check out the morning paper. Our routine had gotten messed up that morning with sick kids and I didn't get my early dose of coffee and gossip. My throat felt a little scratchy and I knew coffee was the fix I needed. I had just taken my first sip when I flipped open the paper that Wren had brought in with him.

"Fuck!" I said when I saw the front-page headline.

"What's wrong," Dare said, running into the room. I held up the paper for him to see "Fuck!"

Wren entered the room next. His eyes rounded in surprise when he saw it too.

"Police Captain Promises to Catch the Christmas Bandits by Christmas Eve," I read aloud. Amazing how Gabe had left that part out, but we hadn't done a lot of talking the night before—well, not with words anyway.

Beneath the heading was a picture of a fierce-looking Gabe taken during the town hall meeting. In comparison to the headline, the rest of the article was tame. Gabe just stated the dollar value of the items stolen or damaged and provided a background story for some of the victims, including myself and Mrs. Hazelbaker who was heartbroken over her stolen sled. Myrna had even added pictures of both our properties to go with the article to give it a personal touch. My heart hurt just looking at the wreaths.

"Shit, look at the wording for the reward! It says a person can earn five thousand dollars if they help 'capture' the Christmas Bandits. Holy fuck!" I exclaimed. "We're going to have a bunch of Dog the Bounty Hunters running around Blissville."

"Has Gabe seen this?" Dare asked.

"He hadn't before I left," I replied. "We were too busy worrying about the babies." I pulled out my cell phone and dialed Gabe.

"What's wrong with the babies?" Dare asked Wren.

"They have colds," Wren answered.

"Oh, I hope Josh and Gabe don't get it too."

"I don't get sick," I told him while waiting for Gabe to answer his phone. My call went to voicemail, which never happened, so that meant Gabe was talking on the phone or busy doing damage control. "Hey, babe, check out the Blissville Daily News if you haven't already seen the headline. Not sure you'll get home at a decent time tonight after all. Love you."

The rest of the salon staff showed up and our day kicked into high gear as people got ready for holiday parties that weekend. Thanksgiving might've been a slow time, but Christmas was crazy busy. Normally, I loved the hectic pace of my job, but I started to feel more and more droopy as the day went on.

The only response I got from Gabe all day was a single word in a text. *Fuck!* The grandmas checked in with me every hour and even sent pictures showing smiling, happy babies. I could tell that they weren't feeling a hundred percent, but were looking a hell of a lot better than they did when I first saw them that morning.

"You don't look so well, Jazz," Mere said when I was sweeping up the hair from my last appointment for the day. She reached up to touch my forehead, but I stepped out of her reach.

"Stay back," I told her. "I think I'm just tired from interrupted sleep, but the twins have a cold."

"You don't get sick," Mere stated.

"I know, but I don't want to take a chance and spread germs to you. It's bad enough that you've been breathing the same air as me all day long."

"Honey, colds are unavoidable. You go on home and let me close up for you."

I wanted to argue, but I could feel a fever coming on. "I'll be better tomorrow," I assured her.

"Call me if you need anything."

I snorted. "With two moms in the house?"

"Yeah, you're in good hands. Let me know how you're feeling though."

I was grateful for the short drive because cold chills had moved in by the time I pulled into the garage. My mom took one look at me and sent me straight to my room.

"I d-d-d-don't get s-s-s-sick," I said through chattering teeth.

She brought me some tea, ibuprofen, and the jar of "goo" to rub on my chest. "You rest for now. I'll bring up some chicken noodle soup in a bit."

"And maybe a peanut butter and jelly sandwich too?" I asked. One little cold had reduced me to a little kid in an instant.

"Of course."

I closed my eyes and didn't wake up again until I felt warm lips press against my forehead. "Hi, baby," I said. I didn't need to open my eyes to recognize who those lips belonged to.

"You don't get sick," Gabe whispered into my ear.

"I don't."

He pressed his hand to my forehead. "Fever's gone."

"Thank God! I hate that our babies felt this miserable. It's horrible. You can't afford to get sick since you only have a few days to catch the Christmas Bandits."

Gabe groaned. "Nothing curbs your snark, does it?"

"It makes me feel alive," I said dramatically. "So, Dirty Harry, what are your plans?"

"Tonight, I'm going to take care of my family."

"Tomorrow?"

"There's only right now," he said, but I could hear his gears grinding. "Hey, I brought up your dinner. Do you feel like eating?"

"Not really, but Mom went to the trouble, so I'm going to give it my all."

"Do you want to eat here or in the sitting area? I can start a fire for you."

"Oh, a fire sounds nice." I waggled my eyebrows suggestively.

"Not tonight, you're in no shape."

"I could totally still rock your world, Gabe," I said, sliding from between the sheets.

"I have no doubt, Sunshine," he said, following me with the tray of food. "Can and should aren't the same things."

"You sound so parental."

"I'm practicing for future conversations with the kids. Is it working?"

"No, I still want you to do me, but I'll be lucky to stay awake long enough to eat my soup."

"I've never seen you sick before," Gabe said worriedly.

"I'll be right as rain in the morning," I promised him.

Gabe set the tray over my lap, and I smiled when I saw that my mom sent up all the things she fed me when I was sick as a kid. Campbell's chicken noodle soup, peanut butter and jelly cut diagonally, lime Jell-O, and a bottle of Sprite. "My mommy loves me."

"She sure does, now dig in while I go check on the babies."

"Bring them to me," I hollered after him, which made me cough.

"I planned on it," Gabe assured me. "I thought we could do story time in here tonight."

I must've been hungrier than I thought because I ate everything on the plate. Maybe that adage about feeding a cold was right, because I felt a little better. I sure as hell breathed better with the "goo" on my chest.

"Daddy! Daddy!" my angels said when Gabe carried them into our room.

He set them down and they tottered their sleepy heads over to where I sat on the sofa.

"I missed you so much today," I said, holding them to me. I kissed the tops of their heads and breathed in their baby shampoo. "I missed bath time."

"You missed a doozy too," Gabe said. An ornery smile crossed his lips and I knew exactly what had happened.

"He said it again, didn't he?"

"Oh yeah." Gabe's lips trembled as he struggled to hold it together. "He got mad when his bath toy was out of reach."

"Dylan James, did you say that naughty word again?"

Our son shook his head.

"I don't think I believe you," I told him. I looked over my shoulder and saw that Gabe was gone. I waited a few seconds then heard the distinct sound of my husband laughing his ass off coming through the baby monitor.

He returned with a stoic look on his face when he rejoined us with a book in his hands.

"That might've worked better had you not lost your sh... cool in the nursery with the baby monitor on."

"Oops," Gabe said sheepishly.

"Read us our story, Big Daddy."

Gabe's deep voice lulled me to sleep long before he reached the end of the book.

SEVENTEEN

Gabe

"MAYBE YOU SHOULD CONSIDER STAYING HOME FROM WORK," I said from bed as I watched Josh get dressed.

"I told you I feel much better."

"Yes, but you also told me that you never get sick. You lied."

"No, it was true at the time, so it wasn't a lie. I can't recall the last time I got sick," Josh countered. "Why are we debating this anyway?"

"I'm just trying to avoid reality for a little longer. Why don't you come back to bed for a few more minutes?" I asked, crooking my index finger at him. "I should take your temperature."

I noticed the extra sass in his swaying hips as he crossed the room. Josh leaned over me, but avoided my greedy hands that tried to tug him down beside me. "You took my temperature once already this morning. Your thermometer said I'm fever free, so I'm going to work." Josh cruelly whipped the covers back, exposing my naked body to the cool air. "Quit stalling and go catch those Christmas Bandits."

I jackknifed into a sitting position, gasping in surprise. "You're so mean." He was definitely going to be in charge of getting the kids out of bed for school someday, especially when they're surly teenagers.

"You haven't seen anything yet, mister." Josh arrogantly ambled away from the bed. "I'm going to need you to capture those bandits like you promised because our family's reputation is at stake."

I recovered my body and lay on my side to watch him finish getting ready. Josh was graceful in everything he did, and I could watch him all day. "I didn't promise to capture the bandits by Christmas Eve," I groaned. "Myrna embellished that part a little bit."

"That doesn't sound like the newspaper editor I worked for in high school."

"People change," I said, shrugging. "Besides, that was…" My voice trailed off when I saw his expression in the mirror.

"Were you about to make jokes about my age? It wasn't that long ago."

"Twelve years," I countered. "People can change a lot in that time."

"So, are you going to argue with me *all* day just to avoid reality?"

"I'd rather fuck, but you insist on going to work," I replied.

"Pretty sure that I know just the thing to motivate you throughout your day."

"Oh, I know you do."

I returned to a sitting position when Josh grabbed the naughty Santa advent calendar off the dresser.

"I knew this would grab your attention," he said smugly. "You can open yesterday's surprise now, but you won't get to use it until you get home tonight."

I rubbed my hands together gleefully. I opened the lid off the box and pulled out a piece of paper. My eyes widened excitedly when I unfolded it and saw the little picture he printed. "A sex swing?"

Josh's face flushed bright red, but I wasn't sure if it was from arousal or shyness. "I, um…" Ah, I had my answer.

I placed my hand on the back of his neck and pulled him to me for a kiss. "Damn, I can't wait to see you in that swing."

"Who said *I* was sitting in the swing?" Josh quirked a brow.

The idea of Josh fucking me in that thing was sexy as fuck until an image of me falling and bringing the wall down with me put a damper on my arousal. "I'm too heavy."

"Nonsense," Josh countered. "It says it supports up to three hundred pounds." He was rocking his poker face and I couldn't tell if he was serious or not. "You hang it from a doorway, which is nice and sturdy." My husband leaned forward and kissed my lips. "I can see you're nervous about the idea, so I'll go first. You can truss me up in that thing and pound the fuck out of me later tonight."

I threw back the covers and hauled ass toward the bathroom.

"Where are you going?"

"I have bandits to catch so I can return home and rock my man's world."

"Alright, team. Let's catch the bandits. We're going to divide up in groups and split the credible leads."

"Define credible, Cap," Adrian said.

"Ones that don't include aliens or famous people," I replied.

"The gypsies are still on the table then?" Officer Jones asked with a snicker.

"Keep it up, Jones, and I'll send you to the surrounding woods to interview Sasquatch."

Everyone laughed, but someone had called the tip line and suggested that Sasquatch was the one waging war on Christmas. I added that one to the Not Likely pile along with Marilyn Monroe and Elvis Presley.

"My apologies. I take it back, Cap."

"Let's see if we can get through half of these tips today and the remaining ones tomorrow," I told them.

"Calls keep coming in, Cap," O'Malley said. "We're getting messages on our social media pages too."

"It'll die down." God, I hoped so.

"Excuse me," a female voice sounded behind me.

I turned around and saw a woman standing in the police station holding her teenage boy in place by the collar of his coat.

"Can I help you?" I asked.

"Yes, I'm pretty sure my son is your Christmas Bandit."

"Come right this way," I said, gesturing toward my office. I really wanted this kid to be the bandit, or part of the crew, but doubted I was that lucky. Besides, he didn't look nervous or defiant—emotions I'd expect him to express if he were guilty. Instead, he looked… bored. He even rolled his eyes as they walked by me.

"I'm telling you, this is your guy," the woman said as soon as I shut my office door. She guided her son to a chair then took the empty one next to him.

"What makes you think so, ma'am?"

"My husband and I caught him sneaking back in through his

window last night after we returned from neighborhood patrol last night," she said.

"Neighborhood patrol?" I asked.

"Sure! They're forming all over town. We want to help you catch the Christmas Bandits."

"You want the money," the defiant teenager said snidely. "You'd give up your own son for a few bucks."

"Try five thousand dollars, but I'd turn you in for free," she boasted then looked at me. "I'm sorry that my son stole from your husband. I'm sure you have techniques to make him tell you where he hid them. I don't mean torture," she quickly said so that I wouldn't misinterpret her intentions. "Lie detector tests or trust serum."

"*Truth* serum, Matilda," the kid said.

"Robert, don't you correct me in front of the chief of police." She glared at her son, but he didn't look in her direction. "And stop calling me by my first name. It's Mom to you."

"He's the police *captain*, Mom."

"Oh you," she growled, swatting her hand in the air. "Anyway, Herb and I looked up and saw a shadowy figure crawl into our only son's window. We rushed inside and found him stashing his load."

"*Loot*."

"Shut it, wise ass!"

It was all I could do to keep a straight face as she butchered slang words and he corrected her. "Loot? What kind of loot?"

"This!" Matilda pulled a baggie out of her purse and dropped it on my desk. "He's been smoking the Sara Jane."

"*Mary Jane*, Matilda. You grew up in the sixties, the best generation for cars, music, drugs, and self-expression, but you don't know the difference between Mary Jane and Sara Jane. Ohhh, perhaps you smoked too much Mary Jane yourself?"

"I did no such thing."

"Me thinks the lady doth protest too much," Robert replied smugly.

"I hate to break up this touching family moment here," I said, interrupting them, "but I fail to see where a baggie with two joints is connected to the Christmas Bandits."

"Where's he getting the money to pay for his drug habit?" she asked me, then turned to face her son. "Care to tell us that?"

"I make ten dollars an hour at the McDonald's in Goodville," he told me. "I'm a recreational user, so I don't spend a lot. Anyway, Captain, they caught me crawling into my window after I had a joint. I'm not your Christmas Bandit."

"It's a pathway drug, Robert."

"*Gateway*, Matilda, and that's debatable."

Then the two of them began to argue back and forth about respecting each other and their spaces. Robert was pissed that Matilda searched his room and turned him in. She burst into tears and claimed she failed him as a mother.

"Excuse me," I said, raising my voice to be heard. "I'm going to confiscate the weed—"

"Hey!"

"Do you have a prescription, Robert?"

"No," he said, slumping in his chair.

"I'm confiscating the weed, as it is still an illegal substance in the state of Ohio."

"You'll probably smoke it yourself after I leave."

Ignoring his remark, I said, "You're free to go."

"Wait! You're not going to arrest him?"

"For what? Two joints? No, I'm not going to arrest him." I took a calming breath before I continued. "You don't have any evidence to connect him to the burglaries and acts of vandalism, so there's nothing I can do on that front either."

"Fine," Matilda said, as she rose to her feet. "I might as well turn over the rest of his drug tools."

"*Paraphernalia*," Robert corrected. "And I don't have any."

"Oh, yes you do! I did another sweep of your room while you were in the shower this morning and found some things we overlooked last night." She reached back into her purse and pulled out a plastic tube and dropped it onto my desk with a *thunk*. "Here's his pipe."

"Oh my God," Robert whined. I never knew a person's face could turn that shade of red. I feared he would combust at any second. "I can't believe you, Matilda!"

"I'm doing this for your own good, Robert. No more pipe or joints."

The red faded from his cheeks and an ornery gleam sparked in his light eyes. "That's not a pipe, Matilda."

"Sure it is." She nodded at me, expecting that I would back her up.

"It's not a pipe," I told her.

"Then what is it?" She picked it up and looked down one end of it. She eased a finger inside it. "It's made from a weird, fleshy rubber."

Robert smiled wickedly, and I could see him mentally counting down for the big moment. Three, two, one… "It's a Fleshlight, Matilda. I use it to masturbate."

"What?" She screeched then dropped it back onto my desk. "When did using your hand go out of style?"

"That's so nineties, Matilda."

"Well," she said huffily. "We've wasted enough of the chief's— um, captain's—time. Let's go home, Robert."

"Take this with you," I said, gesturing to the masturbation device on my desk. "Here, you can carry it out in this." I pulled one of the plastic bags I use to line my trash can from the bottom drawer of my desk. Robert grabbed the bag from me and put his Fleshlight in it. "Don't even think about it," I said when he looked longingly at his confiscated joints.

"You're totally going to smoke my weed," Robert tossed over his shoulder on the way out of my door.

Adrian popped his head in as soon as they left. "Is that what I think it is?" he asked when he spotted the baggie on my desk.

"Yep," I told him. "Mind logging that into the evidence room?"

"No problem," my former partner said. "So, what happened?"

"You wouldn't believe me. Hell, at one point, I thought about calling you in here so you could witness it for yourself."

"Oh, come on, Gabe. It can't be that good."

"Sit down."

I told him the entire story from start to finish, making sure to mimic the tones they used. Of course, I saved the best part for last.

"Fleshlight!" Adrian said, clutching his stomach from laughing so hard.

"Yep! She thought it was his Sara Jane pipe."

"Shut up!" Adrian said through his laughter. "Oh my God."

"You ready to head out and start knocking on some doors?" I asked after he stopped laughing and wiped the tears from his eyes.

"Sure, but your day is going to be a complete downer from here on out."

In relation to the case, I thought he could be right, but I knew there was a very bright spot awaiting me that night. *My Sunshine.* I wouldn't allow myself to think about that or I'd lose my focus.

I saw O'Malley barreling toward us as soon as we stepped out of my office. "Captain, a Channel Eleven news van just pulled in."

"What?"

"They must've picked up the story on the AP wire, or..." O'Malley's words trailed off, but I knew what he was going to say.

Josh! There's no way he would've called his producer and asked them to interview me. No fucking way! Just in case, I called him. "Tell me you didn't do this," I said when he answered.

"Do what?" he asked. He was confused, not playing coy.

"Never mind," I said as the crime beat reporter got out of the

162

van and started walking toward the police station. "I'll tell you all about it—" I heard Josh's muffled voice as he covered the phone to talk to someone.

"Oh my God! Channel Eleven is there?"

"How'd you know that? They just got here."

"My client got a call from her neighbor whose daughter saw the van pull into the station parking lot."

"She called her mom, who called your client, who told you all before the reporter could get inside the building?"

"You've lived here long enough that you shouldn't still be surprised by the speed of gossip."

"Faster than light," I jokingly said.

"News travels fast, bad news travels faster," Josh added.

"Jessica Stanley just walked in, Sunshine. Gotta go. I'll call you later."

"Captain Roman-Wyatt," she said cheerfully as she approached me. "It's been a while. How are you?"

I hadn't talked to Jessica, other than at the corporate events I attended with Josh, since the Broadman case. "I'm doing great, Ms. Stanley. What brings you to town?" I asked like I didn't already know.

"The Christmas Bandits, of course."

"Is crime down that much in Cincinnati?" I asked.

"Hardly, but this story impacts one of our own, so we wanted to do a piece while Josh's show is on hiatus for the holidays."

"It can't hurt," Adrian said from beside me.

"It's good to see you again also, Detective Goode."

"Likewise, ma'am."

"Well, where would you like to do the interview?"

"Do we really have to do this?" I whined.

"Yep, with or without you. Come with me and you drive the narrative, stay behind and there's no telling what I'll do."

"Let's see if we can interview a few of the people impacted by the bandits and perhaps talk to the local businesses who are putting up the reward money."

"Sounds perfect. Maybe we can bait your bandits and catch them in the act."

"Yeah, okay, Daphne. Let's go gather up the rest of Mystery, Inc and get this show on the road."

EIGHTEEN

Josh

"Just a little more to the right, baby," I urged Gabe.

"Here?" he asked, moving his body to the right.

"That's too far."

"Here?"

"Oh yeah! Right there."

Gabe turned away from the ginormous inflatable snow-man he was trying to tether to stakes in the semi-frozen ground. His glare let me know just how much I had irritated him. You damn-fucking-well know that I didn't want that thing in my yard, but it was part of Gabe's sting operation. What punk-ass bandit could resist that big fucker in the police captain's yard? It practically screamed, "Come and get me, fucknugget!" Anyway, if that thing was going in my front yard, then it had to be placed perfectly.

"You're getting even with me, aren't you?" Gabe asked.

"Baby, I have much more creative ways to punish you than have you keep scooting *that thing* all around the yard."

"No, you don't," Gabe returned quickly. "Your methods *encourage* bad behavior. Pretty sure we recently discussed this."

"Do you wish to see my dark side, Gabriel?" I asked, crossing my arms over my chest.

"Hell yeah!"

"You're too eager."

Gabe shrugged. "Hey, you set the precedent, not me."

"It just so happens, I do plan to pay you back for involving our sanctuary in your little scheme."

Gabe crossed the yard and hauled me to his body. "I'm ready right now."

"Follow me."

Gabe didn't do what I said. Instead, he tossed me over his shoulder and bolted into the house, taking the stairs two at a time.

"Be quiet or you'll wake everyone up. They're resting for the big party tonight." Our Ugly Christmas Sweater parties were legendary.

"We have a little time to play around then?"

"How do you have energy to get it up?" I asked. We had taken turns in the swing the past two nights, working through his frustration over the elusive bandits. I was deliciously exhausted and sore in all the right places.

"I'm breathing, aren't I?" The lust in Gabe's eyes sparked need in the pit of my stomach, but I knew we wouldn't have much time before the munchkins woke from their nap.

"Shut the door anyway, because I don't want anyone to hear you shouting," I said, as he carried me into our bedroom.

"Allll right."

"This is not a sexy punishment, Gabe. Your screams won't be from pleasure."

"Oh, you've got me intrigued now."

"Put me down then sit on the edge of the bed." Once he did as instructed, I said, "Now close your eyes and don't open them until I say."

"Yes, Bad Daddy," Gabe purred.

Damn him! "No peeking," I reminded him as I removed my t-shirt and pulled part one of his surprise over my head. I walked to stand in front of him with part two of his surprise in my hand. I held up my arms so his gift was at eye level and tried my best to hold my laughter inside me. "Okay, open them."

"No. I think I'll stay up here tonight."

"What? No!"

"I heard the laughter in your voice and the rustle of you changing clothes in the closet." He reached out and blindly felt around with his hands until he touched his gift. "I fucking knew it was going to be a hideous sweater."

"Duh, it's called an Ugly Christmas Sweater party. Now open your eyes so you can appreciate my genius. We match!"

"No." Gabe lay back on the bed, hiding his eyes behind his forearm. "Nothing you can do will make me acknowledge whatever is in your hands or wear it." He cupped his crotch with his free hand and said, "Well, maybe you could find some way to entice me."

"How old are you?" I demanded to know. *I would not take his bait. I would not take his bait. I would... Damn him.* "Don't get your spunk on my sweater."

"Don't dribble," Gabe suggested, "or, better yet, take the ugly-ass thing off."

"You haven't seen it," I protested.

"Don't need to; I know you."

I was starting to rethink my decision to fall on his cock at the snap of his finger or thinly-veiled challenge. I teased his hard-on through his jeans, as I debated whether I should bring him to his knees with my skillful mouth, or play harder to get. *Yeah right.* I snorted and reached for his top button, but the angry cries coming through the monitor altered my plans.

Gabe groaned in frustration.

"Oh now," I said, climbing off the bed. "It's probably a good thing because you'll want to save your spunk for tonight's gift."

"What time will this party be over?" he groused.

"When the last person leaves." I stopped at the door and looked back at him over my shoulder. "Voluntarily," I amended. "Make sure you're downstairs with your sweater on in an hour."

"Bossy."

"Whiny."

"Horny."

"I'm not touching that one, Gabe."

"You were about to touch it until our precious little angels woke up." I suspected he wanted to use a different noun to describe our children right then, but he was no dumbass.

I left him alone to pout and headed toward the nursery. It sounded like the cries got angrier as I approached. By the time I opened the door, both Destiny and Dylan were wailing at the top of their lungs. I ran to their crib with my heart in my throat, but my fear turned to sadness when I realized what was going on.

"What's wrong?" Gabe asked, rushing into the room. "Uh oh!"

Dylan and Destiny each used one hand to tug a stuffed rabbit between them while they yanked each other's hair with their other hand.

"It's their first fight," Gabe said as we separated the little scrappers. "Do you think it's a sign that they need their own space now?"

"I think so," I replied soberly. The thought of it pained my chest. They were growing up too fast. We were only a few weeks away from their first birthday.

We bounced them against our chests and soothed them, but I was pretty sure that Gabe and I needed to hold them more than they needed to be held. I glanced over at Gabe and saw that he'd already put on his ugly sweater.

"Aww, we're going to look so cute," I said, looking to distract myself from sad thoughts.

"It's not as tacky as I feared."

He looked down at his sweater that had a replica of our home sewn onto it, complete with Christmas lights. I jazzed it up with yard deer, snow globes, and a huge ginormous inflatable snowman that we didn't own. Well, all but one. I didn't know it was a freaking premonition when I made the damn things. Wait! Did I curse us?

"What do these little lights do?" Gabe asked.

"Light up, of course."

"Get out of here."

"Amateur," I said, rolling my eyes.

"How?"

I pushed a hidden button in the center of the wreath on the front door of our sweater. The lights I worked around the house, trees, deer, and inside the snow globe and snowman lit up.

"This is pure genius!" Gabe exclaimed. He reached over and pushed my button so that I lit up too.

Our babies looked at us with wide, wondrous eyes and I worried that they might damage their retinas if they stared too long. At least they forgot to be mad at each other.

"What did you make for them?" Gabe asked.

"Nothing that lights up," I assured him. "That didn't sound

very safe for kids."

"Smart thinking." He grabbed Dylan from my arms and held the little screaming demons close together. The twins stared each other down for a few minutes, and I worried that we were on the cusp of another fight, but then they smiled at one another. "Show me."

"They're more cute than ugly."

"Quit stalling."

"I'm a little nervous," I said, walking to their dresser drawers. "This idea came to me when you started acting like Clark W. Griswold with your quest for a perfect holiday."

"Just show me."

"I have a backup plan."

"I've never seen you so nervous, not even on our wedding day."

"Here goes," I said, pulling one out and holding it up for him to see.

Gabe's eyes widened then he tilted his head back and laughed. "Oh my God! Oh, Sunshine! That's perfect."

I smiled as I looked at the gems I found online. They were white knit sweaters with green and red lights strung across the top and bottom with "Jolliest Bunch of Assholes This Side Of The Nuthouse" stitched in the middle. It looked like something my mom would've cross-stitched back in the day.

"We're going to kick ugly sweater a... butt."

"I can't wait!"

"You sure know how to throw a party, Joshy," my mom said to me a few hours later as we restocked the food on the buffet tables I set out.

I looked around the room at the people I loved most in the world and smiled at their creativity. The ugly sweaters ranged from just gaudy print to reindeer taking a dump in the woods. Some of them were bedazzled with twinkling lights while others played out scenes in movies. There were ridiculous sweaters with Santa smoking a cigar while playing poker and ones adorned with fuzzy white pom-poms to look like snowballs. Our guests were laughing, eating food, and having a great time. It was exactly what the holidays were about to me, and I loved every second of it.

"Thanks, Mama. I get my flair from you."

"You think so?"

We looked down at her sweater that looked like it was knitted with silver and gold tinsel instead of thread. Then we looked over at my dad who wore a sweatshirt with a snowman sewn on the front.

"Yeah, okay," my mom agreed. "I'll take credit for that." She looped her arm around my shoulder and leaned into me. "I never would've thought to give the pets Christmas sweaters too though. That's all you."

"I couldn't let my fur babies feel left out. Diva didn't want any part of her shiny, bling-y sweater, and I have the claw marks to prove it. She sure as hell looks regal in it though."

Buddy seemed to love his reindeer-themed sweater and was as docile as could be when I put the reindeer antlers on his head. Jazzy was too nervous to join a loud crowd, but my furry ferret rocked a snowman sweater in his little sanctuary. The crowning glory were the birds though. Savage rocked his knit sweater that read: Yippee-ki-yay, motherfuckers. Sassy's sweater said: Merry Christmas, you filthy animals. Gabe even taught them a few songs to sing for our guests. Somehow, Savage found a way to put his own twisted spin on things.

"I got your jingle balls right here," Savage squawked from his cage as if he knew I was thinking about him.

"I'm going to miss you guys when we head back to Florida on New Year's Day," my mom told me.

"I'm going to miss you too, but you'll be back for good in a few short weeks. Think of all the fun birthdays and holidays we'll have in this house."

"I never thought I'd want to move back to Blissville once we left town, but no Florida coastal view is more beautiful than my grandbabies."

"I agree with you."

"Why does Gabe keep peeking out the curtains?" she asked.

We didn't tell the grandparents about the setup because one little slip of the tongue at the grocery store would ruin Gabe's sting operation. "Um, he's probably looking out for Santa." We did hire Mr. Adams to show up and pass out the gifts we bought the kids.

"He's like a giant kid at heart, Josh. I just love him to pieces."

Gabe looked over his shoulder and our eyes connected. For that instant, the world faded away. There were no adults dressed in gaudy sweaters or kids running through the house with Buddy chasing after them. The world consisted of Gabe and me. He winked at me then returned his attention to the window.

"Me too, Mama."

I could see disappointment building inside Gabe as the night went on without a single hit to our twelve-foot Frosty out front. He was running out of time to nab the bastards before Christmas Eve.

"Maybe all the publicity scared them into hiding."

"Doubt it," Gabe said. "It's probably because there are too many cars here and they can't be sure when someone will open the front door. I bet they…"

A brain-piercing siren split the air. The dog howled, kids screamed, and the adults pleaded for someone to turn it off. Gabe's eyes widened with excitement as he hauled ass to the front door with Adrian fast on his heels. I knew it was the moment they'd waited for and chased after them. No way I wanted to miss out on the big takedown.

"Hold it right there, asshole," Gabe yelled as he sprinted across the yard chasing after a person dressed in a Santa suit dragging our quickly-deflating snowman with him. The big thing was slowing them down, so they let go to run faster.

"Freeze!" Adrian yelled as he pursued a really tall elf.

Gabe and Adrian performed synchronized dive-tackles to take down Santa and his elf at the same time. The fleeing suspects went down like they'd been hit by those big dudes on one of Gabe's favorite football teams. I thought Gabe called them linebackers, but I called them line dancers to irritate him.

"Yippee-ki-yay, motherfuckers! I told you not to run," Gabe yelled as he pinned Santa with a knee to his lower back while he slapped handcuffs on him.

"Are those candy cane hand cuffs, Cap?" Adrian asked.

Oops! It looked like Gabe grabbed the wrong pair from our bedroom.

"I have the Christmas spirit," Gabe shot back.

"Uh huh," Santa said from beneath him.

"Shut up!" Adrian and Gabe said at the same time.

Two squad cars came flying down the road with lights flashing and sirens blaring. Every neighbor stood in their yard taking pictures or filming the takedown with their phones. They loaded the suspects in the back of the squad cars and then Gabe returned inside with me to comfort our crying babies. Luckily, someone thought fast and unplugged the stupid siren that was connected to the air compressor for big Frosty so that our hearing loss was most likely temporary.

"I'm going into the station for a little bit," Gabe said. "I shouldn't be long." I took Dylan from him and placed him on my free hip. Gabe kissed the babies and me. "I love you guys."

"We love you too. Hey," I said when he started to walk away.

"Don't forget to bring home the candy cane handcuffs." I had planned a fun time with them later.

"I'm never going to live this down at the precinct," Gabe groaned as he walked out of the house.

"My hero," I said to my husband when he presented my stolen wreaths to me a few hours later.

Our guests had gone home, our parents and children had been asleep for quite some time, so it was just the two of us sitting by the fire on the enclosed porch. The only light in the space was the glow from the electric fireplace in the corner, but it was enough for us to watch the snow falling from the sky.

"What did they call their experiment again?"

"W.O.K.E. It stands for War on Kringle Experiment. It was sparked by a comment one of their professors made during a class at Goodville Community College. I guess this guy stated that the world had forgotten the true meaning of the holiday. He was giving extra credit to students who conducted an experiment on what happens when you strip away the commercialization of Christmas, like decorations, Santa Claus, and snowmen."

"You've got to be kidding me," I said. "How the hell did they get away with it?"

"They wore different costumes each time. Turns out that Oprah, Marilyn, Elvis, aliens, gypsies, and even Sasquatch were behind the thefts."

"Oh my God, they're evil geniuses."

"Yeah, and lucky too since none of you are pressing charges now that your belongings have been returned."

"It's Christmas," I said. "It's no time for those kids to spend in jail. Besides, I think we proved just how wrong the nutty professor was. Our community was pissed about our memories and traditions being stolen from us, not commercialized symbols."

"Good point," Gabe said then reached into his back pocket. "I didn't forget." He dangled the candy cane-striped handcuffs from his fingers. "Wanna give these a try?"

"Yippee-ki-yay!"

EPILOGUE

Gabe

EVEN THOUGH OUR BABIES TURNED ONE ON DECEMBER THIRTY-first and January first, we decided to officially celebrate the big day later in January when we could all be together. We had a private celebration with the grandparents on New Year's Eve before they returned to Florida to put their houses on the market. As hectic as Christmas was, it felt great to ring in the new year quietly while our friends traveled or celebrated privately as we did. It was a moment of wonder and excitement over what the new year would bring, but also a little sadness that we couldn't turn back time or hold onto that moment just a little longer. When the clock struck midnight, we kissed our sleeping babies on top of their soft heads before we tucked them into their separate beds. I adored our son and daughter, but I had some adult celebrating to do with their daddy.

Later, I held Josh tight against my chest after I loved him to within an inch of his life. He nuzzled his nose against my tattoo that matched the one on his chest. I couldn't help but think about those empty branches just waiting for apples to be added. I had no idea how many more kids we would have, but I knew it was going to happen when the time was right.

"Give me at least another year," Josh whispered. "Let Dylan and Destiny have two years with Papa and Daddy before they are asked to share."

"Did I say something out loud?" I asked in confusion.

"Nah, I can just hear your gears grinding and took a wild stab in the dark. Lucky guess." He placed a kiss over my heart then said, "Now go to sleep because our little munchkins will be getting up bright and early in the morning. They do not care that it's a holiday and Papa wants his rest to cheer on another football team." I couldn't see his face, but I knew he was rolling his eyes.

"Are you making ribs, mashed potatoes, and sauerkraut?" I asked.

Josh snorted. "Always thinking about your stomach."

"Or my cock."

"It's a tossup which comes first with you."

It was my turn to snort. "Cock then food," I told him. "You satisfied one and now I'm focusing on the other."

"It's New Year's Day, Gabriel. Of course, I'm making ribs, mashed potatoes, and sauerkraut. It's good luck. Now go to sleep."

"Yes, dear."

A few weeks later, I looked around the formal dining room that had been converted to birthday party central. There were balloons, streamers, and colorful banners everywhere the eye could see. "You do realize they're only one year old, right?" I asked.

"Yes, but they'll never be one again," Josh answered.

"What time are the unicorns showing up?"

"Same time as the clowns, dear."

"Snark ass," I grumbled.

"Hey, you're the one who picked this fight. I'm ending it. Quit busting my balls over the babies' big day or I break out the big guns. You should be glad it's too cold for that big blowup jumpy thing that's all the rage or unicorn rides."

"They're strapped in and ready to go," my mom said, encouraging us to bring their mini cakes over.

"I'm not ready for this," Josh whispered.

"The cake mess? I thought you were looking forward to that?"

"No, I'm not ready for this moment to be over. It's happened too fast, Gabe. I swear we just brought them home five minutes ago."

"One breath, one step at a time," I told him.

"Bring those cakes over here, boys. I'm not getting any younger," Bertie said.

"Yeah, we want them to open their presents," my dad said. "No one got arrested over this one."

"Hold your unicorns; we're coming," Josh said. "Get your camera ready. You do photos and I'll do video."

Josh and I placed the mini cakes on their high chairs and we all began singing happy birthday to them. Dylan impatiently grabbed a fistful of cake while Destiny gingerly poked the icing before we finished the final chorus.

I think we snapped a hundred pictures and filmed every second of the cake massacre. Josh made everyone pose with the twins when they opened their gifts so we could put them in their scrapbook. The grandparents made sure that their present was opened last.

"What do you think it is?" Josh asked me. "They seem pretty excited about it."

I just shrugged because I had no idea what was in the big box. "I guess we're about to find out."

My mom pulled off the lid in a dramatic ta-dah fashion, earning surprised looks from Dylan and Destiny.

"Just go with it, kids," I said to our children.

"What's in there, Dylan and Destiny?" Josh asked, sounding more excited than the kids.

Dylan pulled out a stuffed Minnie Mouse and Destiny pulled out a stuffed Mickey Mouse. Destiny took one look at the Minnie Mouse and tossed Mickey to the ground. She reached for Minnie, but Dylan turned his upper body and blocked her.

"No! No!" he said. It was his new favorite word, but we were just glad it wasn't cockbadger.

"Uh oh," I said. "I sense another fight is about to happen."

"Not today," Bertie told me. "Dylan and Destiny, there are more presents in the box."

That settled them down temporarily as they reached into the box once more. They each pulled out a Mickey hat with names embroidered on them and kept pulling them out until there was one for each of the twins, both sets of grandparents, and Daddy and Papa.

"I think we're going to Disney World!" Josh said excitedly.

The final picture of the party was the group of us wearing our hats and smiling for the camera. We set the kids down amongst their new things while we started picking up the wrapping paper mess that was scattered everywhere.

Destiny let out a battle cry worthy of Zena and grabbed the Minnie Mouse from Dylan.

"Fuh nug!" Dylan yelled at his sister.

"Dylan, no!" Josh and I both said at the same time. Our son looked at us like he couldn't understand what the fuss was all about.

"Excuse us a second," Gabe said, grabbing my hand and pulling me out of the room.

He pushed me into the library and we laughed our asses off. Once we gathered our composure, we returned to the dining room. As I passed Savage and Sassy's fancy solarium, I said, "Dirty Bird!"

"Blow me!"

Damn, I had the best life.

The End!

Josh, Gabe, Destiny, and Dylan would like to wish you all a happy holiday! As a thank you for all the love you've shown them, Josh has decided to share a few recipes with his Dye Hard fans. We hope you enjoy them!

JOSH'S RECIPES
Josh's Amazing as Fuck Zucchini Bread

This recipe makes two loaves.

3 cups of flour
1 and ½ cups of sugar
½ cup of brown sugar
1 cup of oil
3 eggs
1 teaspoon of baking soda
1 teaspoon of baking powder
1 teaspoon of salt
1 teaspoon of cinnamon
2 cups of shredded zucchini—Drain excess liquid, but do not pat completely dry. Trust me.
2 teaspoons of vanilla extract (I've also used almond extract)

Here's what you do:

Mix all the ingredients together except the zucchini. It looks a little dry and you're going to wonder why the fuck everyone loves my cooking and baking so much, but trust me. Add the zucchini in last and watch as the moisture gives this bread batter the perfect consistency. If you're so inclined, you can add ¾ cup of nuts to the batter at this point. I'm a huge fun of nuts, but not in this bread recipe. You might like it though.

Grease and flour 2 loaf plans. Bake at 325 degrees for 50–60 minutes.

Gabe likes his slices thick, warm, and with a lot of butter.

Josh's Perfect Pumpkin Pie

This recipe makes one deep dish pie. I double it for two. Please note: don't even think about using the pumpkin pie spice that's premixed. Hell-to-the-no! It is not the same and don't let anyone tell you different! I see you eyeing the cloves and thinking you want to leave it out. Don't fucking do it!

1½ cups pumpkin (small can)
1 small can of condensed milk
½ cup of granulated sugar
½ cup of light brown sugar
½ teaspoon salt
½ teaspoon ginger
½ teaspoon nutmeg
¼ teaspoon clove
1 teaspoon cinnamon
2 level tablespoons of flour
1 tablespoon of melted butter
2 eggs slightly beaten
1 cup of milk

Mix all of that amazingness up and pour it in a deep-dish pie crust. I buy them frozen. It saves time and energy. Yeah, Gabe knows. He's kept my secret all this time.

Below is the critical part in making the pie. Don't screw this part up! It's one thing to leave out the butter, but fucking this step up will ruin the pie. Do you want to ruin the pie?

Bake at 400 degrees for 15 minutes

Reduce temperature to 300 and bake for an additional 45 minutes

If you get carried away with your filling, you may have to bake a while longer. If the center is as jiggly as your aunt Edna's jowls, then you'll need to bake it until the jiggling is gone. I check every two to five minutes.

Refrigerate until completely cool. Now, you can either buy that store-bought whipped crap or you can make my homemade cinnamon whipped cream. The recipe follows.

Josh's Orgasmic Cinnamon Whipped Cream

Recipe yields 1½ to 2 cups

1 cup of heavy cream, chilled
¼ cup of confectioner's sugar
1 teaspoon vanilla extract
1 teaspoon ground cinnamon

Pour the heavy cream into a large bowl (chilled works even better) and beat with an electric mixer until thick and frothy. Add the confectioners' sugar, vanilla, and cinnamon, and beat until medium peaks form.

Scoop that shit on everything!

*You could always add a splash of cinnamon whiskey, bourbon, or a liqueur if you're so inclined.

Josh's Fucktastic Apple Pie—Boozy and Regular

Recipe makes one fucktastic pie.

Regular apple filling:
3 lbs of Granny Smith apples (usually 4 to 5 large apples works well) peeled and sliced thin
½ cup of sugar
3 tablespoons of flour
Pinch of salt
½ teaspoon of each of the following: cinnamon, ginger, and nutmeg (I add ¼ teaspoon of cloves also)
Squeeze of lemon
2 tablespoons of butter

Toss the ingredients together and pour into a prepared pie crust. I use a frozen deep-dish crust. Dot the top of the apples with 2 tablespoons of butter.

Pie Topping:
¾ cup of flour
¼ cup of granulated sugar
¼ cup brown sugar, packed
1/3 cup of butter or margarine, room temperature

Use a pastry blender or fork to mix flour, both sugars, and butter until coarsely crumbled. Sprinkle over the apples.

Bake at 375 degrees for 50 minutes.

Boozy Pie:

To get a boozy pie, simply soak the peeled and sliced apples in the liquor or your choice. Everything else is the same. I prefer to use ¼ to ½ of fireball whiskey then add water until the apples are covered. Let them sit an hour or so in the refrigerator, drain, and pat dry with a paper towel. You might have to add ½ tablespoon more of flour to offset the additional moisture in your apples from soaking them.

The rest of the ingredients and instructions are the same. Top with ice cream or whipped cream.

OTHER BOOKS BY
AIMEE NICOLE WALKER

Only You

The Fated Hearts Series
Chasing Mr. Wright, Book 1
Rhythm of Us, Book 2
Surrender Your Heart, Book 3
Perfect Fit, Book 4
Return to Me, Book 5
Always You, Book 6
Any Means Necessary, Book 7

Curl Up and Dye Mysteries
Dyeing to be Loved
Something to Dye For
Dyed and Gone to Heaven
I Do, or Dye Trying

Road to Blissville Series
Unscripted Love
Someone to Call My own

Coauthored with Nicholas Bella
Undisputed
Circle of Darkness: Genesis Circle Book One

ACKNOWLEDGMENTS

First, I need to thank my husband and children for their constant support and encouragement. It's not easy living with a writer who often disappears into a fictional world for long periods of time. They do so many things to help me out so that I can realize my dream. I love you guys more than words can ever express.

Many thanks go out to my three best friends, Annabella, Deena, and Kerry. They've stood by me, cheered me on, picked me up, and held my hand through some rough patches. I love you girls so very much. I wish everyone had friends like you because the world would be a much kinder place.

To my creative dream team, thanks seem hardly enough for all that you do. Pam Ebeler of Undivided Editing thank you for your tireless work, feedback, and many laughs while editing. Jay Aheer of Simply Defined art is just an incredible artist, and I love how she brings my words to life. Stacey Blake of Champagne Formats is also an amazing artist who does incredible interior formatting and designing for e-books and paperbacks. Let's not forget Judy Zweifel of Judy's' Proofreading. She does an amazing job of finding the tiniest details that make a book shine.

I would like to thank my beta readers for all the honest feedback they give me on my storyline. I appreciate you guys so much. Aimee's ARC Angels are Racheal, Jodie, Kim, and Laurel. Thank you for all that you do!

ABOUT THE AUTHOR

I am a wife and mother to three kids, four dogs, and a cat. When I'm not dreaming up stories, I like to lose myself in a good book, cook or bake. I'm a girly tomboy who paints her fingernails while watching sports and yelling at the referees. I will always choose the book over the movie. I believe in happily-ever-after. Love inspires everything that I do. Music keeps me sane.

I'd love to hear from you.
You can reach me at:

Twitter—twitter.com/AimeeNWalker
Facebook—www.facebook.com/aimeenicole.walker
Blog—AimeeNicoleWalker.blogspot.com